ALONE WITH YOU

HIDDEN LAKE SERIES

D. ROSE

Copyright © 2021 by D. Rose

All rights reserved.

No part of this book may be reproduced in any form or by any electronic or mechanical means, including information storage and retrieval systems, without written permission from the author, except for the use of brief quotations in a book review.

THE PLAYLIST

ALONE WITH YOU

*In loving memory of my grandmother, Edith B.
Thank you for your love, prayers, and support. You are missed so much!*

HIDDEN LAKE

Hidden Lake is located in Flathead county and six hours outside of Billings—the largest city in Montana. It has a population of 15,000 people.

Please note, while Hidden Lake is a real body of water located in the Glacier National Park in the state of Montana, it is not a real city and was created by the authors of this series.

OTHER BOOKS IN THE SERIES

STILL THE ONE BY ASIA MONIQUE
IRRESISTIBLE CRAVINGS BY SHANICEXLOLA

CONTENTS

Chapter 1	1
Chapter 2	11
Chapter 3	25
Chapter 4	35
Chapter 5	45
Chapter 6	53
Chapter 7	67
Chapter 8	79
Chapter 9	89
Chapter 10	99
Chapter 11	111
Chapter 12	121
Chapter 13	131
Chapter 14	141
Epilogue	147
The end	153
Acknowledgments	155
Also by D. Rose	157

CHAPTER ONE

Kiannah

"What have you done, Kiannah?"

This was *just* the reaction I expected from my mother after I removed my hat. With a smirk, I ran my fingers through my freshly cut coils and down the nape of my neck.

"Hi, Dad" I said, ignoring my mother's scowl. After a beat, she stomped away to the kitchen, making me snicker. My dad stared at me with curious eyes, then pulled me into a bear hug.

God, I needed this hug more than ever. I settled into his embrace and inhaled his woodsy scent. He held me tightly for a moment, then kissed the crown of my head.

"How are you, kid?" he asked with a hiked brow.

"I'm okay."

"You sure about that?"

He broke eye contact to look at my hair, making me sigh. My mother's reaction was anticipated, but I never expected judgment from my dad. He was the "understanding" parent; we left the self-righteousness to Mom.

"You like?" I asked with a weak smile. My stomach turned when his eyes narrowed. Once his head tilted slightly to the left, I knew he was psychoanalyzing me.

Here comes the annoying line of questions.

"You want to tell me what led to this? Was it because of mediation today? You didn't call afterward. We were waiting to hear from you."

"Dad," I droned. He threw up his hands and walked away.

It was a haircut, *so what.*

After that happened this past year, they should be happy this was all I'd done.

I exhaled, then attempted to greet my mother, who'd just returned from the kitchen.

"Kiannah, why did you cut your hair? Answer me!" my mother demanded when I reached for a hug. Swatting my hands away, she stepped back and looked at my haircut. Her lip curled and eyebrows furrowed.

Here we go.

"Why would you do this? All that long, thick hair… it's all gone!"

While rolling my eyes, I unzipped my coat and placed it on the arm of the couch.

"Ma, please," I pleaded.

"I can't believe you're acting like a rebellious teenager when you simply could've fixed your marriage."

Yeah, I should've canceled dinner this week.

"Unfortunately, everyone doesn't have the picture-perfect marriage, like you and dad," I sniped.

My heart ached from her hurtful words. However, I didn't let the feeling linger too long before shaking it off. I was more emotional than usual, that was the only reason I allowed myself to even engage this topic. My mother had a sharp tongue. It took a lot of time… and therapy before I learned how to deal with her.

"Marriage takes work! You can't just quit because things didn't go your way. You have so much to learn, little girl."

There's so much you don't know.

With her hands on her hips, she stared at me and waited for my rebuttal.

I had nothing else to say.

Literally nothing.

All the fight I had was left on the table during mediation today. I needed another hug, or maybe an encouraging word from my mother; not her ridicule for wanting better for myself.

She took my silence as a win and walked away. I used the few seconds I had alone to regain my composure. Dinner was going to be tough tonight. Right now, I was the center of attention in my family. In a fantasy world, I would go through this divorce without the scrutiny and unsolicited advice from my family. Their support was enough, but I guess it was too much to ask of them.

After slipping off my boots, I strode to the kitchen to greet my sister, Kym.

"Thanks for having my back," I told her while playfully hitting her arm.

"Wait!" she shrieked, holding up a bowl of batter.

Kym carefully poured the cornbread batter into a cast-iron skillet. She put the skillet in the oven then set the timer. Once she finished, she wiped her hands on her apron.

"I told her it was a trim, but I didn't think you'd go *this* short. What were you thinking, Key?"

I knew Kym had already told her I cut my hair. She and my mother didn't keep many secrets from each other… even if it wasn't their secret to tell.

"It had to go," I replied.

Kym frowned. "I wish there were more I could do."

"You could talk to your girl," I said, referring to our mother. "She doesn't know half the shit I went through with him."

With her back to me, she said, "I'll talk to her."

"Thanks," I replied with a smirk.

"So… how did it go?"

I peeked out of the kitchen to see where our parents were. The living room was empty, so I figured they were in the family room watching TV.

Leaning closer to Kym, I whispered, "It went terribly. Mark is going to make this as hard as possible. He's convinced couples counseling can 'make things right.' It's mind blowing that he's still fighting to be together."

Kym nodded while carefully stirring a pot of cabbage. "We knew he'd act this way, though. So, what's the next step?"

"We have another meeting in a few weeks. After today, I think I'll let my lawyer do all the talking. There's no reasoning with him."

"I think that's best."

Kym handed me a bowl and nodded toward the green beans.

"Did he say anything about the paternity case?"

I finished scooping the last of the beans into the bowl, then walked it across the kitchen to the serving table.

"Nope. I guess we're supposed to act like it isn't happening." I chuckled. "I'm sure he thinks if he stalls the divorce long enough the results would change my mind."

Kym came beside me with a bowl of cabbage. "Do you think the results would change your mind?"

"Not at all."

I'd given Mark more than enough chances to be faithful. It was embarrassing to say how times I'd forgiven his indiscretions. Mark had gotten so used to me letting shit slide, that he didn't even apologize anymore. He'd simply buy me something to pacify me until the next time he cheated. No number of bags or shoes could keep me this time.

"But if you do change your mind, it's okay," she said, thoughtfully. "I'm not saying I'm on his side or anything. I just want you to know that I support you, no matter what."

I knew Kym meant well, but there was no way in hell I was getting back with Mark.

I was done.

"Thanks, Kymmie," I replied, making her smile.

I left the kitchen leaving Kym to finish cooking and plating the dishes. She was weird about people helping her while she cooked. I sat in the sunroom and stared out the large casement windows. My sister's backyard faced the mountains and it looked especially mesmerizing in the fall.

Every fall and spring, Mark and I visited his parents' cabin in the mountains. Whenever we were on the rocks, we'd go there for a week to reconnect. I knew it was a temporary fix to an ongoing problem, but I still looked forward to spending time with him. It was rare for me to have his undivided attention.

"Dinner will be ready soon," Kym said, snapping me out of my thoughts.

I nodded, still staring ahead. The longer I stared, the faster my heart beat. It didn't matter how much of a sore spot the mountains were, I couldn't look away.

"I have to tell you something," she said.

This time I turned to face her. My eyebrows furrowed once I met her gaze. Kym's cocoa brown skin flushed as she gnawed on her bottom lip. My stomach turned as I waited for her to speak.

"What did you tell mom?"

She hummed. "So, I accidentally told her about the house."

After jumping to my feet, I stalked over to her. "What? Kym, how could you?"

I balled up my fists as heat consumed me. "You promised! Remember the 'sister code' bullshit *you* created?"

"I-it just came out."

"Like everything else, right?"

I knew she'd tell our mother about my haircut, I didn't care about that. But when it came to our relationships, and finances, we kept our parents out of it.

"Key, I'm sorry. She asked if I'd been lonely while Everett was away, and I mentioned you slept here last week. One thing led to another...I didn't mean to tell her about the repairs, and you thinking about selling it."

While running my hands over my face, I pushed out a breath.

How could she do this to me?

Kym grabbed my arm and squeezed it tightly. "I told her not to say anything to you."

"Yeah, like she'll listen."

"She will," Kym assured. "And if she doesn't, I'll step in."

I wanted to believe Kym. She wanted to earn the role of the protective big sister, but how could she protect me when she was the cause of my problems?

"We'll see," was all I could muster up.

The sooner I got through this dinner, the sooner I could go home.

An hour into dinner, Kym had dominated most of the conversation. Our dad loved her fiancé, Everett, and his stories about being a traveling agriculturalist. Just when I thought I was in the clear, our mother swiftly changed the subject.

"You've been awfully quiet, Kiannah," she said, cutting off Kym. Dad shot her a look that she ignored. "Do you regret cutting your hair, yet?"

I chuckled. "Not at all."

I'm counting down the minutes until I leave.

Kym made my favorite dessert, pineapple upside down cake. I knew it was her way of making up telling Mom my business. And I was going to take full advantage of her guilt trip. Half of that cake belonged to me.

"Why'd you do it?" she pressed.

"Because I needed a change, Ma. I'm 29 years old and I've never cut my hair."

Dad cleared his throat and reached across the table for my hand. "Is that the only reason?"

And I was repulsed by the look in Mark's eyes when he saw me today.

Mark *loved* my hair.

It was sickening how enamored he was with my thick tresses. I made the mistake of wearing my hair in tousled curls, his favorite. During the entire mediation, he practically drooled from across the table. I was so pissed by the end of our meeting; I had to do something, anything to make me feel better. So, I called my stylist and begged her to squeeze me in this afternoon.

Several hours later, my hair had been cut into the cutest tapered pixie, with highlights. There wasn't enough time to style my hair, so I opted to wear my natural curls.

Meeting my dad's intrusive regard, I replied, "That's it."

Mom sighed. "Well, I hope you're happy with your decision. It seems you're making a lot of them without even thinking things through."

"Mom," Kym warned.

Our eyes met as I swallowed the lump in my throat.

"No, Kymberly. Your sister needs to hear it."

"Hear what?" I asked, my heart beating a mile a minute.

"You are so spoiled and stubborn. When things don't go your way, you quit. So what you and Mark were having problems, you could've worked through it. You didn't fight for him or your marriage. And now you're selling your dream home? What's gotten into you, Kiannah?"

"It's really none of your business what I do with my house or marriage."

"Key," Dad warned.

"Oh really?" Mom shot back. Kym reached for Mom's arm, and she jerked it away, making me chuckle. "Someone needs to tell her that this isn't who she is!" Mom waved her hand and twisted her lips.

"Irene!" my dad's voice shook me to my core. It was rare for him to raise his voice, but it was needed at this moment. Had he not intervened, who knew what would've been said. "You've gone too far," he said after a beat.

Silence loomed over us for a moment. Kym stared at me with worry etched on her soft features. I was too upset to say anything else to her. Heat coursed my veins as my mother's cruel words set in. After wiping the corners of my mouth, I stood from the table. Without another word, I left dinner. I turned off my phone before leaving Kym's to avoid calls from her and Dad.

The thirty-minute drive gave me all the time to think about the last five months of my life. I went from being happily married–even if it was a delusion–to being a soon-to-be-divorcée with no support from my family. Kym understood my decision, but I knew she was against it. Every chance she got, she asked if I was "sure" about the divorce. She adored Mark just as much as Mom, plus he and Everett were friends.

By the time I made it home, my head pulsated from all the thoughts racing my mind. I didn't bother to turn my phone back on. After taking a long, hot shower, I laid down.

As I laid in my towel, curled in a ball, I let out a wail. I hadn't realized how badly I needed to cry until I wiped away my last tear. I grieved the end of my marriage, the toxic relationship I had with my mother, and the lack of support I had from my family.

For months I'd been trying to keep it together. I couldn't show any signs of sadness about the end of my marriage because my family would tell me to forgive him. It wasn't about forgiveness; it was about deserving better. After wiping away the last of my tears, I finally turned my phone on. As expected, I had several voicemails and texts from Kym and Dad. I rolled my eyes before scrolling to read a text from my best friend, Alex.

```
Alex: Kym called and said you needed
me. I'll be there next weekend!
```

I couldn't help but grin from ear to ear because Alex would do more than be there for me. She'd remind me who I was before I got married. That was the part of me who needed nurturing.

CHAPTER TWO

A *fresh start.*

That's how my brother, Paris and sister-in-law, Opal, proposed I move in with them; by offering me a fresh start.

I wasn't too sure if living in the Middle of Nowhere, Montana would feel fresh, but I didn't really have a choice. There wasn't much time to consider my next move when they called, so I accepted their offer.

The idea of living somewhere different excited me. Something about packing up every six months and finding a new home was thrilling. I'd lived in every place I dreamed of as a kid. From Italy to Morocco to Spain to Portugal; I'd experienced new cultures, ways of living, and stretched my artistic capabilities. It was a euphoric feeling that I never wanted to live without.

However, this move didn't have the same sentiment. As we drove down the curvy roads covered with tall trees, I had the urge to capture the foliage surrounding us.

This isn't research for work.

The realization had me pushing out another sigh. I should've taken the spark of inspiration as a good sign, but instead it made me wonder when my career took a turn.

It took a turn when you missed your deadline four times.

I shouldn't have taken the deal.

My agent and I knew I needed more time to plan and execute the book, but greed got the best of us. Seeing a five-figure advance with my name on it made me lose all sense. Now, I was on pause.

Pause.

Every time my agent said that word, I got hot. I knew my book wouldn't see the light of day if it were up to them. It left me wondering if I should scrap it all together and start something new.

Something fresh.

The change of scenery captured my attention as I straightened my posture. My brother's house was like something out of Architectural Digest. I knew this was all Opal's doing. Loved my brother, but he didn't have an eye for design.

So, this is my new home?

My eyes widened and a sigh fell from my lips.

"Were you expecting something else?" Paris taunted after pulling into his driveway.

"Nah."

"Still mad, huh?"

"Hell yeah! You could've been on time," I groused.

"I told you we got caught in traffic," he explained while killing the engine.

I was too tired for his shit, so I dropped the topic, and

exited the car silently. It had been two days since I slept in a bed. The thrill of hopping from flight to flight had fizzed. My back was sore from sleeping in those uncomfortable chairs at the Airport. I wanted nothing more than to take a hot shower and sleep.

"The guest house is all yours," Opal said, patting my back. "Come on. Let me help you get settled."

"Nah, I got it, O. You've done enough. Just point me in the right direction."

"You sure?"

I nodded. "Positive."

Opal shook her head. "You and P can be so stubborn sometimes. Go through the living room, and out the back door. The door is unlocked, and your key is on the coffee table."

That was all I needed to hear as I made my way through their living room. I peered around their cabin styled home and smiled at the photographs covering the walls. On their coffee table, next to my set of keys, was my debut book, a collection of photographs I'd taken while living in Spain. My brother was a pain in the ass, but he supported me like no other. After grabbing the keys, I continued to the guest house.

"Aye, Man," Paris called out from the back door. "I'm happy you came."

Glancing over my shoulder, I replied, "Me too."

"Hopefully, you'll stick around for a while."

I chuckled. "We'll see."

Paris remained in the doorway until I made it to the guest house. Before closing the door, I gave him a nod that he mirrored.

Home sweet home.

Opal had the guest house looking like a suite at The Four Seasons. I wasn't surprised that she pulled this space together in under just a month's time. What was once a storage room for my brother was now a fully furnished studio apartment. I dropped my luggage at the door and walked around. The fridge was stocked, the closet was filled with fresh linens, and there was a 65-inch TV hanging over a wood burning fireplace.

Maybe this wasn't a bad move after all.

After a short tour, I showered then unpacked my bags. It was no point in leaving my stuff in suitcases any longer. I didn't have much to do since Opal had already hung the majority of the clothes that I sent ahead of time.

What she didn't unpack, she meticulously placed in the closets. Once my clothes and shoes were organized, I sat on the foot of the bed. From the corner of my eye, I saw my camera bag across the room. My stomach turned as I tried to remember the last time I'd used my camera.

Three, maybe four months? Damn.

While shaking my head, I begrudgingly went over to get it. I pulled out my memory cards first, then I searched for the adapter. After connecting the adapter to my laptop, I inserted the card. As soon as the images loaded, regret washed over me.

I wish I'd been honest with my former publisher sooner.

They'd given me every opportunity to share my thoughts on book two to no avail. My agent, Loren, suggested that I follow their lead this time around because they compromised *so much* during the edits of my debut release. My gut told me not to do it, but I was so eager to please *them*.

Taking Loren's advice backfired when the first prints were due, and I had nothing to send them. I was too insecure that the photos I'd taken didn't fit their vision to show them. I'd internalized all of their critiques about my first book, and it took a toll on my mental.

According to their research, my readers wanted my next book to be less portraits, and more architectural structures. Also, I was given a deadline I knew I couldn't meet. Three months wasn't enough time to capture the essence of Lisbon.

Before doing a series in a foreign country or unfamiliar city, I do some research too. Each place became a home to me, an expedited timeline didn't allow me the chance to fall in love. I should've spoken up instead of succumbing to the pressure of meeting the reader's exact needs. Because of my inability to advocate for myself, my career was suffering.

I looked at a few more pictures, stopping on one that brought the fondest memories. The portrait of a tawny colored woman with a radiant smile brought up fond memories of Lisbon.

Her.

Nalia Silva, my friend and sometimes lover, was the hardest part of leaving Lisbon. During my stay, she showed me the beauty of Lisbon through the eyes of the Afro-Portuguese community. She was the inspiration behind the series I *wanted* to do six months ago. Not only did I fail myself, but I also failed her.

Before I got too carried away with regret, I closed the

laptop. I promised her I wouldn't mourn the end of our relationship. We understood that our time together was temporary, but dammit if I hadn't fantasized a different ending.

I laid back on the bed and let my mind race with thoughts of her. Before her, I had no interest in falling in love. My camera was the love of my life, and nothing could come between us, until her. She opened my eyes to the beauty of love, and what could come from it.

Nalia's gentle approach to love made me question how I loved, romantically and platonically. She was another reason why I decided to move with my brother. I needed to mend our relationship. We had avoided the issue long enough; it was time to heal those wounds.

As I laid in the dark, I thought about how long I would stay. I needed to stay long enough to get closer with Paris, but I didn't want to become antsy. My career also needed a serious revamp. That couldn't happen in the Middle of Nowhere, Montana. I needed somewhere exotic to spark my creativity. I needed a muse. The mountains and lake weren't enough.

My racing thoughts weren't enough to keep my eyelids from being heavy. The weightier they became, the less I fought to stay awake. It wasn't long before I succumbed to sleep.

LIGHT TAPS against the glass door stirred me from my nap. Blinking my eyes, I peered around the dark room. After stretching, I turned on the lamp on my way to the door. Opal waved a bowl of chili underneath my nose, making my stomach growl and mouth water. Opal knew her way around the kitchen, which was another reason why I moved with them.

"Hungry?" she asked with a grin.

I chuckled. "Starving."

Stepping aside, I gave her space to come inside. Opal walked over to the kitchen area, and put the bowl in the microwave. I took a seat at the table while the food warmed up.

"When was the last time you ate something?"

While shaking my head, I replied, "You don't want to know."

Opal scowled. "I came right on time then, huh."

"Yup."

A beat passed before she sighed. "So, I know you hate surprises…"

"What did he do now?" I asked. My heart thudded and heat coursed my veins.

"Paris wants you to come to the Oak Bar tonight. He's arranged for you to have a VIP booth, food, and bottles. The whole nine."

The microwave chimed, giving me some time to gather my thoughts.

He knows I won't tell Opal, "No."

My eyebrows met. "If there's anything I hate more than surprises, it's the club. You know I'm not going, right?"

Opal brought the bowl over, then sat down across from me. "Come on. It'll be fun."

Since I was too busy stuffing my face to reply, I shook

my head. Opal eyed me in a way that reminded me of my mom's scowl.

She waited for me to finish chewing then said, "Paris has been planning this since you agreed to move in with us. He just wants to show you how happy he is that you're here."

"He couldn't take me out to dinner or something?"

Through giggles, she replied, "Nope!"

My shoulders dropped from the deep sigh I pushed out. I continued eating the chili and weighed my options.

If I go, I won't be there long. Maybe for an hour or two.

Opal must've read my mind, because she broke the silence to say, "Just go for an hour. Thursdays usually aren't busy, so don't worry about it being crowded. And Paris won't hover, I made him promise not to."

"Fine," I conceded.

Opal clapped her hands while cheesing. "Great! We'll leave in an hour."

———

I CAN'T BELIEVE *I agreed to this shit.*

Opal undersold The Oak Bar's traffic on Thursday nights. The line for general entry was wrapped around the building. My stride slowed as I took in the bustling scene. Opal reached for my hand and tugged me to the front door.

"Mrs. Jarreau, your booth is ready for you, and Memphis. Follow me," the waitress said, as we entered the lobby.

Opal scoffed. "Violet, I told you to call me Opal. P knows I hate being called that by y'all."

"I know, I know. He told us to call you Mrs. and to remain 'professional' at all times,"

Opal rolled her eyes while laughing.

We strode through the lobby to an elevator just before the dance floor. Violet pressed the up button, then turned to me.

"You must be Memphis, the baby brother," she teased. Her eyes lowered, and a smirk formed on her lips.

I chuckled. "That's me, but as you can see there's nothing baby about me."

Violet bit her bottom lip, trying her hardest to hide that she was blushing. She recovered quickly, then replied, "Paris has told us so much about you. I hope you enjoy your celebration tonight."

I shot her a polite grin. "I'm sure I will."

From my peripheral, I noticed Opal's smirk. Once we reached the top floor, Violet exited first. Opal waited a second before following suit.

She nudged my side, then said, "Paris has a strict policy about mixing business and pleasure."

"She came onto me," I defended while grinning. Opal squinted her eyes, silently scolding me. "I won't make any promises, but I'll *try* to behave."

"Boy!" she yelled, while hitting my shoulder. Her hit gently pushed me out of the elevator and into the VIP area.

Violet ushered us to our booth where bottles of champagne were already chilling on ice. While Violet and Opal had a side conversation, I made myself comfortable.

I stretched my arms along the back of the sueded booth, and peered around the room. Thankfully, it wasn't too crowded up here. Paris knew how much I hated crowded spaces; it was partly why I didn't go to clubs or lounges. His attention to detail meant he was just as invested in fixing our relationship. I didn't need VIP booths at clubs to know he loved me, but I appreciated the grand gesture.

"Let me know if you need anything," Violet said to me before leaving.

I stared at her, noting the fiery look filling her brown eyes.

I can think of a few things you can help with...

"Will do," I told her.

My gaze followed her curvy frame until she disappeared down the flight of stairs across the room. Moments later, my brother stopped by to "check" on me, and Opal.

"Y'all good?" he asked with furrowed eyebrows.

Opal nodded, then accepted a chaste kiss on the cheek. "I didn't know if you preferred light or dark," he said to me. "So, I told them to have the champagne ready. I remember you liking the gold bottles." Paris smiled nervously. I'd never seen my brother like this before.

I held up my hand. "It's cool, P. This is more than enough, bro."

"You sure?"

"Positive."

"I'll take a French 75, and an order of truffle fries," Opal interjected.

Paris looked at her and smiled. "I got you, baby. I'll be back in a few."

She pressed her hand against his chest. "Take your time. We'll be fine."

"Okay, okay," he said before leaving us.

Once he was gone, Opal leaned closer to me. "It's time to loosen you up."

My eyebrows met. "I'm chillin'."

"And that's the problem. Shots will do the trick," she assured me. Not even a minute later, Violet returned with three shots on a tray, and a bowl of sliced limes. Opal took two of the shots off the tray and handed one to me. I assumed the last one was for Violet. "Wanna toast to anything special?"

"To *loosening* up," I teased.

Opal laughed. "Cheers."

We tossed back the light brown liquid that I realized was reposado tequila. I grabbed a lime and sucked it, hoping it would make the shot less intense.

"Another?" Violet asked while collecting our empty glasses.

"We're good for now," Opal told Violet, prompting her to make an exit. "See this isn't so bad," she said to me.

With a shrug, I replied, "It's cool."

Opal rolled her eyes. "You're so nonchalant… about everything."

Ignoring her remark, I changed the topic. "Paris has come a long way from his dive bar days."

"He has!" There was a spark in Opal's eye. She was just as proud as I was about Paris's growth as a business owner.

The Oak Bar wasn't like the sports bar he once owned. From the oak-inspired décor to the dress code, this place was on its way to being upscale. Judging by the long line, it was obvious Hidden Lake was in need of a place like this.

"I need to run to the bathroom," Opal told me while standing up. "I'll be right back."

I nodded, then continued to vibe to the music.

While Opal was gone, Violet brought Opal's drink and food. She lingered for a bit, busying herself with opening the bottle of champagne for me. After filling a flute, she handed it to me.

"How long are you in town?"

"What happened to being professional at all times?"

Violet rolled her eyes. "I was schmoozing," she droned.

After taking a sip of the semi-sweet drink I replied, "You know I can't fuck my brother's employee, right? Not good for business."

"What makes you think it's not good for business?"

"Because shit like that gets messy."

I made that mistake long ago, when I was much wilder, and dumber. It caused a rift between me and Paris when his best bartender quit because of me. At the time, I didn't realize how my selfishness affected his business.

"It won't get messy. I'm not like that," she retorted.

My eyebrow rose, and a half-smile formed on my lips. "I didn't say you were. I just know how shit like this ends. It's not worth it, love."

Violet smiled. "How will he ever know?"

Looking past her, I saw Opal returning with two other women behind her.

"Opal," I replied simply. "She sees everything."

She turned and met Opal's pensive stare. I held up my hands expressing my innocence.

"Memphis, I ran into my soror, Alex, and her best friend, Kiannah in the bathroom. I met Alex in college after she transferred. Do you mind if they join us?"

My gaze swept over Alex, then Kiannah. Both were fine as hell, making my decision an easy one.

"Not at all," I told her while moving over to make room for them. Kiannah scooted in first, then Alex and Opal followed.

"Can you bring us two more glasses, a bottle of Casamigos Reposado, and shot glasses, please?" Opal asked Violet.

"Sure. I'll be right back." Violet excused herself from our table, making room for Opal and her friends.

"So, Memphis," Alex said once they were seated and settled. "Opal tells us you just got in from Portugal?"

"Yeah, I was out there working on a project that fell through."

Opal scoffed. "He's being modest. Memphis is a published author and photographer. He's staying with us while he figures out his next move. Remember that book I kept telling y'all to buy?"

Alex's eyebrows met while jogging her memory. "Oh yeah! Shit, I ain't know he was this fine. Let me order a copy, then. Key, you want one too?"

Kiannah giggled. "Sure."

I chuckled, then replied, "Thanks. I appreciate the support."

"Of course!" Alex pulled out her phone and placed an order on the spot. Violet returned with the glasses, then poured champagne for the ladies before refilling my glass. This time she didn't linger. I suspected it had everything to do with the glare she got from Opal.

"Y'all from here?" I asked, looking at Kiannah.

She sipped her drink before answering me. "Yup. Born and raised."

"She left for college, though. I still don't know why she came back," Alex added.

That made Kiannah smile... her smile made my chest tighten. My gaze met her lips, then her eyes that remained on me too long for my liking. She crossed her legs, causing her dress to rise a bit. My eyes fell to her thick thighs, forcing a sigh to fall from my lips. I looked away, hoping no one caught my reaction. From the opposite side of the booth, I peeped Opal's smirk. She nodded approvingly then ate a French fry.

Opal peeps everything.

"Opal! This was our song back in the day!" Alex shouted when "Bad and Boujee" came on. She didn't give Opal a chance to react before pushing her out of the booth.

"You don't wanna join them?"

Kiannah shook her head. "Nope. That's a song they used to stroll to in undergrad. I'll be Bad and Boujee, right here. If that's okay with you?"

That's more than okay with me.

CHAPTER THREE

Memphis

"If you're gonna stay here, you have to take a shot with me."

Kiannah winced, while shaking her head. "Hard pass. I barely wanted to come out tonight."

"That makes two of us. Why didn't you want to come out?"

She shrugged. "Just not in the mood to party. But when Alex is in town, partying is a *must*."

I nodded. "I feel you. This isn't how I thought I'd spend my first night here. My brother is the owner of this place. He and Opal set this up for me."

"That's sweet," she mused. "Where did you live before coming here?"

"I was in Portugal for a little over six months."

Her eyes ballooned, and lips parted. "Wow."

Before we could get into why I left Portugal, I turned it back on her. "Alex here for a special reason? Or just because?"

Instead of answering right away, she looked away

while gnawing on her bottom lip. A few seconds ticked by before she said, "Maybe one shot isn't a bad idea."

My eyebrows met. "Why?"

"Because I can tell we're about to have one of those "deep convos." It'll require some liquid courage to open up."

I poured our shots, then handed her a glass. She looked at the glass with a scowl.

"Don't get scared now," I said to her.

"Who's scared?" she asked, gaze leveled.

"Aight, then."

We tossed them back, and I waited for Kiannah to speak.

"Well, she's here because I'm going through a divorce. Last week, I had my first mediation with him since we separated, and it didn't go too well."

"Damn, I'm sorry to hear that."

But happy to hear you're single-ish.

"Don't be sorry," she said, waving her hand.

"How long have y'all been separated?"

"Ten months. I *finally* filed about two months ago." She sighed. "I'm *so* happy that it's almost over."

I smiled. "In that case, congrats. Can't say I feel bad for dude, though. He definitely fumbled the bag."

Kiannah laughed while pushing my shoulder. "Can't lie. He did."

"I'm already knowing," I told her as my gaze swept over her.

"Anyway," she droned, while running her fingers down the nape of her neck.

I stared at her and waited for her eyes to meet mine. It

didn't take long. When our eyes locked, Kiannah licked her bottom lip before capturing it with her teeth. Her sienna-colored skin flushed, and eyes flitted.

"So, you're a photographer, huh?" Kiannah asked.

"Yup. In high school, I started taking pictures of my friends, and family. From there, it became a passion, and now it's my career." I held out my arm to show tattoos on my inner forearm. Kiannah's soft hands grabbed my arm and pulled me closer to her.

She smiled softly. "This is cute. I want a tattoo, but I'm too scared it'll hurt."

Kiannah examined my tattoos carefully, while tracing her fingers over the aperture tattoos near my wrist.

"These didn't hurt too bad. What would you get?"

With a shrug, she said, "I don't know. Something girly, like a butterfly or something."

"You know butterflies symbolize change?" I asked with hiked brows. "It would be fitting considering your current situation, and all."

Kiannah's eyes narrowed, and head tilted slightly to the left. She looked at my arm again, like she was seriously considering getting a tattoo.

"We'll see. I'd have to get it here," she said, rubbing my aperture tattoo. "So, I can see it often."

"I agree."

Kiannah released my arm and grabbed her champagne. "What made you want to publish a book?"

Her innocent question made my heart drop.

Just answer the question.

"After years of working freelance, and building a solid portfolio, my mentor encouraged me to enter a competition. My career was kinda at a standstill, and I needed more exposure. I wasn't too confident I'd win, but I did. The prize was a book deal, an agent, and money of course. I ended up using the prize money to get a lawyer to read over my publishing contract," I added while chuckling.

Kiannah's eyes were wide. "Wow. And here you are being all modest about it."

I shrugged. "It's not that big of a deal."

"Are you serious? It's a huge deal!"

It was a huge deal. It's over now.

"You know you can publish independently, right?" she asked.

"Nah. It's too expensive."

Kiannah's eyebrows wrinkled. "So, you're giving up?"

Running my hand over my face, I sighed. "I don't know what I wanna do, right now. Hopefully, I'll figure it out while I'm here."

She nodded, then sipped her drink.

We bobbed our heads to the music and watched the people around dance. A few songs later and her question was still on my mind. Publishing independently crossed my mind a time or two. However, the costs of printing, marketing, and a tour changed my mind. My second book had to get the same red carpet treatment as my debut, and I wasn't ready for all that responsibility.

I needed to come up with a plan, and quickly.

"You know Opal and Alex aren't coming back anytime soon, right? Alex loves to dance," Kiannah said, halting my racing mind.

I looked at the small crowd in the middle of the VIP

section. It took a second, but I found them dancing. Opal saw me looking and waved for us to join. While shaking my head, I mouthed, "I'm good."

She rolled her eyes in response, then went back to dancing.

"It's cool. I'm probably gonna leave soon," I told her.

I'd kept my promise and stayed well past an hour. The bar was getting more crowded, thus my anxiety was kicking in.

I stared at Kiannah for a beat, contemplating if I was *really* ready to go. She met my gaze with an intense one of her own. I was enjoying my time with her and didn't necessarily want it to end.

She could leave with me.

Nah, I just met this woman, and *technically*, she's married. Plus, I didn't need to be starting anything new right now. I didn't know how long I'd be here, and certainly didn't have the time to commit to a new situation.

It could be just a one-time thing.

"So, you're gonna leave me here, all alone?" she asked, poking out her bottom lip. Lust flickered in her brown eyes, making heat spread across my chest.

"What would you say if I asked you to leave with me?" I shot back, meeting her fire with fire.

Kiannah cleared her throat. "I'd say how soon can we leave?"

After retrieving my phone from my pocket, I said, "I'm ordering our ride now."

"I'll let them know," she said, nodding toward Opal and Alex.

I knew Opal would have an earful for me in the morning. However, those worries were out shadowed by the desire to have Kiannah, even if it was just for tonight. While she told them we were leaving, I ordered a ride, and shot Paris a text.

While waiting for Kiannah to return, I realized I might've been regressing by taking home a woman I'd just met. This was a habit I hoped to have left in Lisbon.

I didn't want to set myself up for something I couldn't commit to in the end.

"Opal is gonna take Alex home, and Paris will pick Opal up from there," she said when she returned.

"Cool."

Twenty-minutes later, we were back at my place. Kiannah kicked off her heels, and sat on the couch, while I got us bottles of water.

"I hate wearing heels," she said, sighing.

I smirked. "You looked good in them, though."

Kiannah grinned. "Gee, thanks."

Her phone chimed, stealing her attention. She sent a few messages, before turning her phone on vibrate.

"Alex made it home safely. I'm sure she's going to have a lot to say about me leaving her tonight." She looked at me with a smirk. "Nothing bad, though. It was her mission to meet someone new."

"Mission accomplished," I replied, handing her a bottle of water.

She drank her water, while peering around the room. "Are these your photographs?"

With a nod, I said, "Yup. I didn't notice them earlier. I guess I was too tired."

Kiannah walked over the photographs that hung to the right of the fireplace. They were from a black & white series I did while visiting Chicago several years ago.

"They're amazing. You captured Chicago beautifully."

I stood beside her, smiling wide. It had been a while since I got to witness a reaction to my work.

"Memphis," she said softly.

It was the first time she'd said my name all night. My heart thudded against my chest.

Turning to her, I replied, "Yes?"

I grabbed her chin and tilted her head back to meet my gaze. My eyebrows drew together, when she refused to look at me.

"If you're not ready, there's no pressure," I told her after a beat.

I didn't consider that I might've been the first man she's been with since her separation. If she wasn't ready to go there yet, I understood why.

"It's not that."

"Aight. So wassup?"

Kiannah peered up at me, an innocent smirk resting on her full lips. I pushed out a slow breath when she took a step closer, eliminating the space between us. After wrapping her arms around my neck, she leaned upward, brushing her lips against mine. My hands found her waist, pressing her petite frame into mine. Our lips met for a slow, lazy kiss. For seconds we kissed without urgency. She sucked and nibbled my bottom lip, making me groan throatily.

"I've been wanting to do that all night," she whispered against my mouth.

I kissed her again, this time with vigor. My tongue pushed between her lips and met her tongue. Our bodies pressed into each other as my hands slid from the small of her back to her ass. She smiled against my lips, pleased with the firm hold I had on her. We stopped kissing long enough to make it back to the couch.

Kiannah pushed me on the couch and straddled my lap, surprising the shit out of me. The sweet, reserved woman from the club had taken charge of the situation. And I liked that shit. Cupping my face, she kissed me, deeply.

"Where are the condoms?" she asked, then sucked my lip painstakingly slow.

Condoms, where did I put them?

My mind was mush.

"I'll be right back," I told her, tapping her hip to move. In record time, I grabbed a condom from the bathroom, and returned to Kiannah, who was laid on the couch in nothing but her bra and panties.

Damn.

Pulling my shirt over my head, I tossed it aside, then unbuttoned my pants. Kiannah watched intently, making me move faster to get to her. She spread her legs enough for me to get between them. I stared at her ankles and kissed my way to her thighs. I slid her panties over her hips, and down her legs, licking my lips at the sight of her pretty pussy.

I should've been surprised by how badly I wanted her. I'd met this woman a few hours ago, and all I knew was that she was going through a divorce. And all she knew about me was that I was a struggling artist. Those complicated facts didn't mean much at the moment.

Kiannah grabbed the condom off the coffee table and opened it. After sheathing myself, I slid into her wetness. We moaned in unison as I rocked into her.

Shit.

Her tightness, and wetness had me damn near speechless. My eyebrows wrinkled, and my bottom lip tingled from biting down so hard. I was trying to keep it together, trying and failing. A low, throaty groan expelled from my lips when she hooked her leg around my waist.

"Memphis," she mewled, making my heart thud. "Deeper," she begged.

So, I gave her what she wanted, longer and deeper strokes. Her nails dug into the flesh on my shoulders, and moans grew louder.

"Like that, baby?" I asked, against the shell of her ear.

"Yes," she breathed, then captured my lips with hers. Between her tight pussy, warm kisses, and moans, I was on the brink of cumming, but not before her. "Don't stop," she pleaded while wrapping both legs around my waist.

"I got you," I assured her.

She continued to moan as I trailed kisses down her neck and collarbone. Moments later, she released a breathy whimper, and she held me tight.

There it is.

Shortly after she peaked, I did the same.

After cleaning up, and disposing of the condom, we spent the next hour or so on the couch in silence. I wasn't sure how this would play out in the morning, but I didn't dwell on it too long, though. Kiannah lay on top of me, her warm soft skin covered in goosebumps as I caressed her arm. Lifting her head from my chest, she looked at me. I met her inquisitive gaze, then kissed her forehead. She tilted her head up, giving me access to her soft lips. I pecked her a few times before devouring her lips. Moments later, my dick was hard and ready to please her again.

And I did just that, until we were too spent to move.

Several hours later, I awoke alone in my bed. The sun shone through the windows, making me squint. Turning over, I grabbed the note she left on the pillow.

That was fun. Let's do it again, maybe? – Kiannah

I chuckled. "Yeah, we'll see."

CHAPTER FOUR

Kiannah

You are too grown to be sneaking home.

I couldn't do anything other than laugh as I brushed my teeth. I'd successfully snuck home at six this morning without waking up Alex's nosey ass.

Me, sneaking into *my* home was hilarious.

But it was totally worth it.

Butterflies took flight in my belly from the mere thought of the night I had with Memphis.

Back to reality, though.

Unfortunately, that reality included emailing my lawyer before spending hours in my basement designing and pressing custom T-shirts for my dad's bowling team. After showering and getting dressed, I went downstairs. In the kitchen, Alex was making us breakfast. I took a seat at the kitchen counter, ready to eat her delicious pancakes.

"Well, look who snuck in at the wee hours of the morning!"

My cheeks warmed. "Oh, shut up!"

Alex snickered, then continued to tease me by handing me a cup of coffee, while saying, "I'm sure you could use some caffeine."

"Thanks," I droned, accepting the cup. I took a sip and moaned. "When did you go to Maia's Sweet Treats?"

"While you were in the shower washing away your sins."

I nearly choked on my drink, messing around with Alex. "Can you please relax?" I asked, between giggles.

Nope. I'm getting these jokes off," she said while flipping blueberry pancakes. "But seriously, you okay?"

"Never been better," I replied.

I wasn't sure if it was the post-dick glow, or what, but I was feeling much better compared to a few days ago.

You still haven't told me why Kym felt the need to call me?"

Rolling my eyes, I sipped more of my toasted latte. I hadn't spoken to my parents or Kym since dinner. And I didn't plan on talking to my mom anytime soon. We needed some time to cool-off.

"Mom and I got into an argument at dinner."

"About Mark?" she deduced.

"Yup. She's still mad about the divorce. She says I'm too stubborn and spoiled to work things out with him."

Alex scoffed while sliding a plate with pancakes, eggs, and bacon across the island to me.

"You'd think Mark was her real son with how hard she's going for him."

"Right," I said, between bites. "I'm trying so hard to not put all my business out there because she doesn't even know the half."

Alex joined me at the kitchen island with her plate. "And the wild thing is, if she knew everything he'd put you through, she'd be embarrassed by how she's been acting."

It was true, but she wouldn't be half as embarrassed as I was for putting up with his bullshit.

"I guess we'll never know, huh?"

Alex stopped eating. "Why not? Key, you're not the one who's the villain here; Mark is. Stop protecting him."

"I'm not protecting him," I defended.

Am I?

"So, why haven't you told your parents that he cheated on you and *might* have a baby on the way?"

I tried getting advice from my parents the first time he cheated. I often replaced the terms mistress and cheating with work, just to protect my ego. My parents didn't question it because they saw how hard he worked. Their advice always suggested I was doing something wrong, which made me put a guard up.

"Because," I droned, trying to think of reasons. "It's complicated," was what I settled on after a beat.

Alex rolled her eyes and continued eating.

The sound of my phone ringing brought me momentary reprieve. My stomach churned when I saw it was a call from my lawyer's office. I guess she wanted to talk about why I didn't want to move up our next mediation.

I knew it was Mark trying to buy time while waiting for his mistress to give birth. He hadn't shared the due date, but I knew it was any day now. We separated shortly after he broke the news to me. He begged me to stay with him until after the birth, but I couldn't do it. I couldn't ignore the possibility of my husband starting a family with someone else and sticking beside him. Especially when I'd wanted to have a baby, and he said, "It wasn't the right time."

"Kiannah, I have some news to share, and an email wouldn't be appropriate," my lawyer, Suzanne said.

"What did Mark do this time?" I asked, hopping down from the barstool. My heart raced as I strode to the office.

Suzanne sighed. "He has decided to forego mediation and sign the papers."

A smile formed on my lips, and my eyebrows wrinkled. While I was elated to hear this news, I was left feeling unsettled.

"What made him change his mind?"

"This is the part I didn't want to email. The paternity case is closed, and the results came in, and he is the father."

My stomach turned and the taste of bile filled my mouth. I paced back-and-forth in the office while holding my forehead.

What the fuck?

I didn't want it to be true. A small part of me wanted to believe that he didn't father a child with another woman, but here we were.

"Kiannah, you still there?"

After clearing my throat, I said, "Uh, yeah. I'm still here. What are the next steps?"

"We just need his signature, and we're good to go. He's also agreed to all your terms, so won't have to worry about how to divide y'alls assets."

Thank God.

This is the seamless divorce I wanted from the beginning. No fighting, no courts, just signing the documents and parting ways, peacefully.

"Thank you so much, Suzanne."

"It's been my pleasure, Kiannah. I'll have my assistant arrange a meeting sometime next week, sound good?"

"Yup. See you then."

After ending the call, I jumped up and down while shrieking. I guess my shrieks sounded like cries, because Alex rushed in the room with a scowl.

"Are you okay?"

I pulled her into a hug. "I'm better than okay! Mark has agreed to sign the papers!"

"What?" she asked, shaking my shoulders. "I can't believe he changed his mind."

The reason why he changed my mind had me releasing Alex, and sitting down on the bench next to my desk.

"Yeah, he got the results back from his paternity case."

Alex nodded, already knowing what that meant.

"That bastard." She shook her head, then took a seat next to me. "I know that shit was hard to hear," she said, wrapping an arm around my shoulder.

It felt like a slap in the face. Granted, I had no business trying to have a baby with a habitual cheater, but the naïve part of me thought it would strengthen our relationship. Who would've thought that a baby would be the reason I left Mark for good? After every infidelity, Mark swore those women meant nothing to him. He swore he used protection every single time too.

Bullshit!

Life had a funny way of showing you people's true colors.

"Well, we have to celebrate him signing them papers!" Alex said before singing Usher's song, "Papers."

I chuckled dryly. "The last time I went out with you, I left with a stranger."

"I mean, it sounds like you should be thanking me. You woke today with a little pep in your step, and you just got some bittersweet news. I don't know, Memphis might be good luck."

Alex's ability to always find the bright side of things was… interesting to say the least. But her words did have me wondering if I was ready to date again. Since my separation, I'd gone on two dates. Both were terrible, making it easy for me to put the brakes on dating until my divorce was finalized.

Slow down, sis.

I didn't even know if Memphis was interested in anything beyond last night. Now, I regretted leaving that note.

I probably seem thirsty as hell.

"When are we gonna do the shirts?" Alex asked, oblivious to the thoughts running through my mind.

"Right now," I told her. I needed to do something to get my mind off the divorce, Memphis, and everything in between.

A SMILE SPREAD across my face as Alex held up the final versions of my dad's bowling team's shirts.

He's going to love this.

"So, when are you going to stop playing and make this a real business?"

"It is a *real* business."

I had the documents and bank account to prove it.

"I mean, like brick and mortar, and not your basement. You barely have enough space to work down here." Alex looked around the basement.

I'd created a workstation for my iMac, t-shirt press, and other necessary equipment to run my business. The space had gotten a little crowded over time, but I wasn't ready for a bigger space. That would require more money, and way more responsibility.

"This space is enough for the time being."

"If you say so," she said in a singsong tone. Alex hummed, then moved on to folding the next shirt.

An hour later, the shirts were ready for delivery. I scheduled the drop off before my mom got home from work. I didn't feel like arguing with her today, especially since I was sitting on good news. When we arrived at my parents' house, my dad was in the garage, loading his car for tonight's game.

"How's it going, Kid?" he asked before kissing the crown of my head.

"Hey, Dad."

Our greeting was brief because he was eager to hug his "favorite" daughter, Alex.

"Papa West! It's been too long," she said, hugging him tightly.

I rolled my eyes. "It's been three months," I retorted, smirking when they shot me a glare.

"Don't hate because I'm his favorite," she goaded.

My dad chuckled. "How long are you in town?"

"Just until Monday. I had to check on my sister." Alex nudged my side, making me giggle.

"We appreciate you visiting every once in a while. I'll have to tell Irene to cook before you leave."

Alex and I looked at each other.

"It's too short notice," she said, shooting me another look to which I shrugged.

"No, it's not. Irene would love for y'all to come over." His eyes were fixed on me. "You need to talk to her, Kiannah."

"Dad, you know she's not ready to have a civil conversation yet."

Or ever.

It was only a matter of time before he brought up dinner. My mom and I would have a fight, a few days would pass, then he'd tell me it was time to bury the hatchet. We never actually would bury the hatchet, though. This was our cycle. it wasn't ideal nor was it healthy, but I'd come to accept it over time.

"You still have to try. How about y'all come over sometime over the weekend, and I'll have her cook. Y'all can talk then."

Alex cut in. "We have a pretty busy weekend packing orders and doing other stuff."

My dad's eyebrows met. "Stuff like what?"

"Brunch with my Soror."

My heart dropped to my stomach.

"When did you confirm brunch with Opal?" I interjected.

Alex pursed her lips together. "Not too long ago."

Before or after I fucked her brother-in-law?

My dad watched silently, reminding me that he was the master at reading body language. So, I quickly regained my composure and smiled.

"Well, Dad. We don't want to hold you up. Here are your shirts." I handed him the bag they were in. "Talk to you later, and good luck tonight."

"Thanks, Kid. See you later. I'll call you later to further discuss this *thing* between you and your mother."

We shared an embrace before parting ways.

The moment Alex and I were out of the neighborhood, I asked, "Brunch with Opal?"

She burst into a fit of giggles. "I swear I wanted to tell you earlier, but then your lawyer called."

"Alex," I whined.

"Come on, it'll be fun. Plus, Opal is a good host, and a great cook."

"Alex, I had a one-night stand with her brother and left the next morning without a word." Well, I left a note. A note with *no* contact information; not even an Instagram handle. I really was a newbie in these dating streets. "No amount of mimosas and shrimp and grits will make up for shit being awkward."

Alex grinned. "It won't be awkward. He wants you to come."

"What?" My eyebrows furrowed as I fought the urge to smile.

"Yeah. When Opal told him about the brunch, he asked if she was inviting you too."

My cheeks warmed and my heart fluttered.

"Like I said, no awkwardness, just a good time that might end with mimosa dick." Alex looked at me impishly.

I wanted to address her "mimosa dick" remark, but I was too busy thinking about Memphis. My mouth watered as I thought about his charming smile, thick beard, and beautiful molasses colored skin. While I *thoroughly* enjoyed the sex, I was more interested in talking to him. Memphis's laid back demeanor made it easy to open up. I hadn't expected to share my relationship status, but something told me I could trust him with such information.

Unlike the other guys I dated, he didn't see me as damaged goods. He *congratulated* me; something I wasn't used to hearing at all. It was that moment; I knew I was going home with him. It sounded cliché, but Memphis was different. I couldn't put my finger on how just yet.

However, I was interested in finding out.

CHAPTER FIVE

Memphis

I leaned down, holding onto my knees for support as I fought to catch my breath. My heart pounded against my chest, and beads of sweat ran down my forehead. I remained in this stance for a few seconds, then continued running.

Paris is trying to kill me, man.

It was lowkey embarrassing that I was getting smoked by my brother, who was five years my senior. I wasn't surprised, though. He was the recipient of the Doak Walker award during his college days and was a top prospect for the NFL. His career came to a halt after suffering a life-threatening concussion. It wasn't an easy decision, but he forwent playing in the NFL and attended grad school instead.

He glanced over his shoulder. "Keep up, baby bro," he said, sounding perfectly fine.

Meanwhile, I was fighting for my life back here.

When he realized I wasn't going to catch up, he slowed down his pace. Once I caught up with him, we stopped running. I took the break as a chance to catch my breath. Taking another deep inhale, I exhaled slowly with my hands on my waist.

"I thought you said you were in shape?" Paris asked in between slow, deliberate breaths.

While shaking my head, I replied, "I said I work out from time to time. Running three miles has never been a part of my regimen."

Paris chuckled. "It will be soon. Come on."

I let him go ahead of me, unconcerned with how fast he was running. I hadn't run in months, and even then, it was a quick mile just to get the blood flowing. Three miles was insane. Once I finally caught up with Paris, he was at the top of a hill overlooking mountains in the distance. The view was beautiful.

I wish I had my camera.

"You see that peak over there." Paris pointed. "That's Heaven's Peak. A little ways over is Mount Vaught, then Stanton Mountain."

"How do you know all this?" I asked, still in awe at the view.

"A friend of mine named Lawrence works for the Glacier National Park Museum, he gave me and Opal a tour a while back. I know where all the mountains and peaks are located along this trail."

I nodded. "It's nice out here, man."

"It is. Opal used to run this trail with me, but she stopped after a while. She says I run too fast."

Wiping away the sweat on my forehead, I replied, "She ain't lying."

Paris chuckled. A beat passed, then he asked, "You ever

thought about taking pictures of stuff like this?" I shrugged. "I know it's not as exotic as Portugal or Spain, but I'm sure you could capture the beauty of Hidden Lake."

"When did you come up with this idea?"

"Not too long ago," was his answer. "Lawrence will be at brunch if you wanna know more about the area and the museum. He'll be happy to help."

I appreciated my brother for trying to help, I really did. But something told me he was doing damage control for our dad.

"You know I met with mom and dad while I was in New York, right?"

Paris nodded. "I know, man."

My dad and I had an interesting relationship. As long as we didn't discuss my career, we were good. Of course, that wasn't often, we stayed at odds. To him, photography was just a glorified hobby. Even after I got my deal and published a book, he remained firm in his stance. He couldn't wait to say, "I told you so," when my deal fell through. My parents drove all the way from Upstate New York, during my layover in Queens, just to tell me I should've had a back up plan.

"He told me not to come here and spend all your money. And that I needed to find a real job, soon," I told Paris. "Why can't he just support me? Is it so hard for him to admit he was wrong?"

Paris kissed his teeth. "He's just old school and set in his ways. Don't let that stop you from following your passion. It's work for you this long, why does it bother you so much now?"

I pushed out a breath while pinching the bridge of my nose. "Because he's not like this with you." His eyebrows shot up. "And I have to deal with the constant comparisons like you're the blueprint or something."

I thought I'd grown out being jealous of Paris and my dad's relationship. Sitting across from my dad as he went on and on about the success of Paris's business opened an old wound. A wound that didn't heal easily. It didn't matter to my dad that I was more successful than Paris at one point. I even helped with their bills for a period of time because I could. It hurt that he refused to acknowledge how far I'd come.

Paris patted my shoulder. "It's fucked up when he does that, and I've called him out on it. However, I don't want you to think I'm exempt from his ignorance. We didn't talk for almost a year after I went to grad school."

My eyes widened as I folded my arms over my chest. "What?"

"Yeah, man. I didn't tell you because I didn't want you to pick a side or get caught in the middle, like Mom."

I cast my gaze to the ground as I thought back to when Paris went to grad school. Around the same time, I had moved from our hometown, Port Arthur to Los Angeles to be a freelance photographer. My dad wasn't happy about the move, but he didn't dwell on it too much. Now, I knew why. Once they reconciled, he turned his frustrations on me, and I'd been getting the brunt of it ever since.

"Going back and forth only feeds his ego. You have to be okay with your choices, and not need validation from him."

"Aight, I hear you."

Paris had a point. The only reason my dad and I got into it was because I wanted him to see my point of view.

"What did Mom say about all this?" Paris asked, making me laugh.

"Man, she was talkin' about it's time for me to settle down and start a family."

"So, the usual?" We laughed.

"She thinks I'm just out here wildin' in every country I live in."

Paris smirked. "I mean, you didn't waste any time when you got here."

"Yeah," I drawled.

There wasn't much I could say in defense. I knew it looked bad, especially since Paris was privy to my old ways. Ways that involved starting things and leaving them unresolved. I didn't have those intentions when I got here, though. It just happened.

"So, that's it?" Paris asked with a hiked brow, resembling our dad.

I shrugged. "I don't know yet."

"Opal told me she's going through a divorce. You sure that's something you want to get involved in?"

Here comes the judgement.

"Don't start," I warned. "We're grown and knew what we were doing that night.

"I don't know, man. She's going through a divorce, and I hear the dude is giving her hell."

The only person I would have this conversation with was Kiannah. If she wanted me to know the details of her divorce, she'd tell me.

"What does that have to do with anything?" I asked. "

He eyed me for a moment. "It could be a toxic situation. I'm not tryna tell you what to do, but just be careful."

I nodded. "I got this man."

Paris started walking in the opposite direction of the trail we ran to get here.

"Where are you going?" I asked, following behind him.

"Home. This is a shortcut." He chuckled, I assumed from the scowl on my face.

"You don't need to worry about me. I can handle myself."

Paris nodded in response. "Okay. Just a head's up, Opal invited Alex and Kiannah to brunch. I didn't think it was a good idea."

"Yeah, we talked about it. I want her to come."

Paris grinned. "Ah, I see what's going on."

"What?"

"This is like your last situation," he admonished. "You tried a relationship with the first person you met in Portugal. And you see how that ended. I hope you learned from your mistake."

Paris's account of my last relationship was a little warped. Our relationship wasn't a "situation;" there were real feelings involved. Yes, I met Nalia my first night in Portugal, but it took a minute before we were together officially. While he was happy to hear I met someone, he didn't like the age difference. I wouldn't expect Paris to understand how I fell for a woman fifteen years my senior. But it happened, and I wouldn't let him reduce what we had to just a one-night stand.

"It's not the same," I countered, not really trying to get into it with him.

I wasn't sure where things were headed with Kiannah, but I knew I liked her energy. The details of her previous relationship weren't important right now. I could use a friend who could relate to being in a space of newness. After talking to Kiannah, I got the sense that she understood me.

"If you say so," Paris replied, after a moment. His eyebrows furrowed and mouth twisted. I knew he wanted to say more but didn't want to risk starting an argument.

The remainder of our short walk was spent in silence, giving me more time to think. I still wasn't over the view my brother showed me today. My mind whirred with ideas of capturing the peaks and mountains in the area. Landscape photography wasn't my specialty, but I was up for a new task. I had a few more days before I had to call Loren. She wanted to shop around for a new deal, but I didn't have anything to pitch at the moment. The longer I took to come up with something, the longer I'd be without a deal.

"You two were gone longer than expected," Opal said once we got back home. She was in the kitchen cooking with Anita Baker playing in the background. "Brunch starts in two hours, and. There's still so much to do."

Paris groaned while ascending the stairs to shower. I lingered in the kitchen area with Opal.

"You know you don't have to do this," I reiterated to Opal. She rolled her eyes and continued cooking.

I appreciated her for wanting me to meet their closest friends, but this was all too much. Plus, I was beat from running three miles in the woods with Paris's crazy ass.

Opal sighed before saying, "Memphis, I want to do all this. The sooner you meet some people, the sooner you'll feel at home."

"I do feel at home."

"Good. I would ask if you're excited for today, but clearly you aren't." Opal eye's narrowed.

I smirked. "With the way you're in here throwing down, you know I'm ready to eat."

"You're always ready to eat," she said with an eye roll. "I'm talking about mingling and making friends."

"You know if Alex and Kiannah are coming?"

She grinned. "Yes. Knowing Alex they'll probably be late. But go on and get dressed. We're eating promptly at one!"

"Got it," I said, walking over to the refrigerator for water. Before leaving the kitchen, I turned to Opal. "Thank you… for all of this."

"Anything for my favorite baby brother."

"You're *only* brother."

I knew how badly she wanted for me and Paris to fix our relationship. If she hadn't intervened a few months back, we probably wouldn't be talking, still. Not only was Opal Paris's voice of reason, but she was also mine too. I had a soft spot for her because I'd always wanted a sister. So, despite me not wanting to be social today, I'd suck it up for Opal.

CHAPTER SIX

Kiannah

Alex looked at me, a smirk rested on her lips while holding up her mimosa. I returned a grin just as wide before tossing back the last of my drink. She was right about Opal's cooking, it was bomb. If I ate another morsel of food, the button on my jeans would've popped.

I peered at the end of the table where Memphis was seated. He was too busy talking to see me staring at him. Between the music and other conversations occurring, I couldn't hear him. I was sure Paris and his friends were asking Memphis about photography.

Earlier, I saw him pointing at his tattoos, reminding me of the conversation we had at the club. I was seriously considering getting a butterfly on my wrist. However, I needed to get the courage to ask him to join me. It seemed silly and too soon to ask. I'd only known him for four days.

Four days.

And after day two, I was ready to see him again. It was

ridiculous how eager I was to see him. I brought my flute of champagne and peach juice to my lips. The sweet, fruity bubbles fizzed on my tongue. We hadn't been able to talk yet because Alex and I got here just as it was time to eat. I didn't know the brunch was for *him*. Everyone was pulling him in a million directions vying for his attention.

If I could just get his attention.

"You okay, Kiannah?" Opal asked while refilling my glass. She smiled sweetly and waited for my response.

I nodded, then sipped my drink. "I'm good. Everything was delicious, by the way."

"Aw, thank you. There's plenty of food, if you want more."

Holding my full belly, I replied, "I'm stuffed. I can't eat anything else."

Ppal continued refilling everyone's glasses, and I returned my attention to Memphis. Our eyes met, and he smirked, making my stomach flip. He nodded toward the kitchen, then stood from the table. I waited a beat before doing the same. Luckily, Paris had everyone's attention as he told a story about hiking with Opal.

Everyone's laughs faded as I rounded the corner to the kitchen.

"Hey, you," Memphis crooned, making me jump. I recovered just as he wrapped his arms around my waist.

My arms wrapped around his neck as our bodies collided. "Hey. You're pretty famous around these parts," I teased.

He loosened his hold on my waist but remained close to me. I moved away from the doorway to the kitchen island. Just to give us a little space. Memphis looked good and smelled even better. He must've been wearing the same cologne that he wore at the club. It was masculine and warm, a chill shot down my spine.

"I'm glad you came thru," he said. "I ain't know if it was too soon to see you again or not?"

Shaking my head, I replied, "It's not."

"What are y'all doing after this?" he asked. "I want to show you something."

"I have to take Alex to the airport in a few hours, that's it."

"Cool."

Memphis took a step closer, planting his hands on the counter behind me. His cologne filled my nostrils after I inhaled deeply. My heart stopped momentarily when he leaned down, aligning his lips with mine.

"We should get back to the dining room. I mean, you are the guest of honor."

They can wait," he said before kissing me. After indulging in a deeply passionate kiss, he stepped back, giving me time to catch my breath. "You go first," he told me while walking in the opposite direction.

I nodded, then returned to the dining room. Everyone had left the dining room and went to the family room, except for Alex and Opal. They were talking quietly when I entered the room and stopped when they heard my footsteps. Alex exhaled when she saw it was me.

"What were you and Memphis doing?" she asked, wiggling her brows, and grinning.

Rolling my eyes, I said, "Talking. What are y'all over here whispering about?"

"Alex thinks Lawrence is cute," Opal crooned.

"Lawrence?" I asked, confused because he wasn't Alex's type at all.

She typically liked guys who were assholes.

Alex laughed. "I know, I know. He's not my type, but I gave him my number anyway."

"Sometimes change is good," Opal told her. "Paris and I took a chance moving here four years ago, and it worked out for us. His lounge is doing well, and I just got a promotion at my job. We didn't know what to do in Chicago after grad school."

Listening to Opal talk about her and Paris's journey to Hidden Lake made me think about me and Mark. I was once hopelessly, and deeply in love like them. Mark and I moved here shortly after getting married to be closer to our families. He was estranged from his parents, but still wanted a family unit nearby. My parents happily took him in, to the point where they became overly protective of him.

I guess Alex was right when she said I was protecting him by not telling my parents the truth. Our family dynamic had changed so much this year, and my parents were struggling to accept he wasn't a part of the family anymore. But I couldn't continue to coddle him when he was the reason our lives changed.

"What's on your mind?" Alex asked with wrinkled brows. Opal left the living room a few moments before to check on the other guests.

I chuckled. "Listening to Opal made me think about me and Mark."

Alex hugged me. "Aw, friend. It's gonna be okay."

Her hug was right on time. I hated how these feelings came out of nowhere. The sadness, uncertainty of my future, and guilt of breaking up my family were all weighing me down. But I had to remain strong because I deserved better.

"Come on, Memphis is about to show everyone the pictures he took in Portugal."

Alex changed the subject.

I followed her to the family room where everyone was seated on their plush couches, watching Memphis set up his laptop to the projector. I found space next to Trinity, Opal's best friend on the couch and Alex sat on the floor in front of me.

Memphis stood in front of everyone with his arms folded over his chest, smirking.

"I'm only doing this because Opal and Paris have been asking to see them since I got here. I took these photos in the beginning stages of my second book. It's not what my former publisher wanted, but I thought I captured Lisbon in a way no one else could."

He started the slideshow and spent time explaining the details behind each picture. From restaurants to family dinners to parks to markets, Memphis made us fall in love with Lisbon. It felt personal. I didn't know much about photography or publishing, but I knew his pictures were beautiful. Once he reached the end, he stopped on a photo of a woman. She was gorgeous. Memphis stared at the picture for a beat, then looked at me.

"I wish I could take full credit for the pictures I just showed y'all. But it was this woman who introduced me to Lisbon. I'm glad I got to capture her home through her perspective."

Everyone clapped, except for Paris. He excused himself and Opal followed behind him.

"What are you gonna do with these pictures, man," Lawrence asked.

Memphis shrugged. "I haven't decided yet. They might stay in the archives."

"So, you have more to show us?" Trinity asked with wide eyes. "I mean, if everyone has time."

Memphis laughed. "I have to find the memory cards first. Maybe another time."

"He's not gonna show us all his pictures for free, guys. Order a copy of his book to see more," Opal interjected when she got back. I noticed Paris was still missing in action. She looked at Memphis and nodded toward the left. I wondered what they were silently communicating.

Lawrence interrupted them by saying, "Well, I have to leave, but I'll be in touch with you, Memphis. We could use your work in our museums. And there's never been an exhibit for Hidden Lake. I really believe you could be the one to do it."

Memphis smiled, and I swear my heart stopped for a second.

"Sounds good to me, man," Memphis replied before shaking his hand.

Opal and Memphis walked Lawrence out leaving me with Alex and Trinity.

"I can't believe we've never met before," Trinity said to me. I learned that she worked for the same company as Mark and Everett. She didn't work in the same department as them, but I didn't doubt she knew who they were. I wasn't going to ask her though. The less people who knew about me and Mark, the better.

"I know. Whenever I meet new people, I'm always reminded that Hidden Lake isn't as small as I think it is."

Trinity smiled. "I know right. It only feels small when you're dating."

"What do you mean?" Alex asked with wrinkled brows.

"It just seems like everyone is dating the same people. Especially at my job. There are so many office flings it's ridiculous."

My stomach knotted, and my mouth went dry. I knew too well about the flings that occurred at her place of work. My soon-to-be ex-husband was one of the main culprits.

Alex rolled her eyes. "Ugh. Don't get us started on that shit."

Trinity laughed. "Girl, I won't because I have a few horror stories myself. It's crazy how easily people get caught up at work. One of my good friends just went through a paternity suit with our coworker. He wanted to keep it under wraps, but everyone knew. It was a mess."

Alex and I shared a look.

This sounds familiar.

"Are they still together?" Alex pressed.

I knew she was dying to know if this was about Mark or not. I, on the other hand, didn't want to know. Trinity seemed cool, and if she was tied to him in any way, we couldn't be friends.

Trinity laughed. "They were never together. He was

only in it for the sex, but she didn't want to believe it. He refused to be a part of the child's life without a paternity test. They spent the entire pregnancy arguing about getting a test done. She made him wait until the baby was born, he was on pins and needles the entire time."

"Niggas ain't shit," Alex mused.

"No, she ain't shit. The baby wasn't even his."

We all laughed. "I don't feel bad for him," Alex said.

I nodded while silently thanking the Lord I wasn't the subject of their office gossip.

"Not at all," Trinity confirmed. "I'm only dating long distance these days. Can't have office drama or any drama really, if you're not in the same state."

Alex nodded. "I feel that."

The conversation shifted to Alex's online dating experiences, and I silently excused myself. I wasn't in the mood to hear those stories again, especially since I didn't want her horror stories to deter me from dating. I wandered through halls, heading toward the formal living room. Memphis had to be around here somewhere. I was ready to see whatever surprise he had for me.

"You gotta let that hurt go," Paris said.

"Hurt? You're the one who stomped out over a picture of *my* ex."

My eyebrows shot up.

The woman in the portrait is his ex?

I wasn't bothered by that fact, but curiosity got the best of me as I listened to the brother argue.

"Because she used you, and you're too naïve to see it."

Memphis chuckled. "How did she use me, Paris? She

didn't gain anything from helping me with that series. The pictures never got published."

"She knew you would bring business to her father's failing restaurant."

I assumed Paris was referring to the restaurant from the slideshow. His accusations were a little far-fetched. It sounded like he was more upset that Memphis was with her at all.

"The minute you lost the deal, she was gone."

"That's not what happened, man. We were over long before that happened. I just didn't tell you."

I stepped back quietly, feeling guilty for eavesdropping. This wasn't how I wanted to hear about Memphis's past relationships. I walked the opposite way and didn't stop until I reached the kitchen. Opal was putting away food, stopping when she heard my footsteps.

"I think the brothers are arguing," I told her.

She nodded. "They can never be nice for long. Did you have fun today?"

"I did. Please invite me to every brunch or dinner party you have in the future."

Opal laughed, then agreed to keep me on the guest list. We exchanged numbers and promised to meet up in the upcoming weeks. Moments later, Memphis stormed into the kitchen. His demeanor changed when he saw me.

"Busy?" he asked me, his eyes begging me to say "No."

Behind him was Paris who looked just as annoyed as Memphis did seconds ago.

"Lead the way," I told him.

We walked to the guest house; Memphis seemed preoccupied with his thoughts until we got inside.

"You okay?" I asked after a beat.

Memphis shook his head but didn't say anything. He went to his closet and pulled out a frame from the top shelf. Walking it over to me, he handed me the matte black frame that held a picture of a butterfly.

"I found this yesterday and thought of you."

"Did you take this picture?"

He nodded. "Yeah, when I was living in Brazil. I was trying something new, but it didn't work out. Nature shots aren't my thing."

My cheeks warmed. "Aww, thanks. I'm gonna hang it up as soon as I get home."

I stared at the orange and black butterfly for a moment, grateful for the second chance I was getting soon. My meeting with Suzanne was scheduled for Friday, and I couldn't wait to pop a bottle to commemorate my divorce.

When I looked up, Memphis was staring at me, his dark orbs were filled with lust and wonder. Heat coursed through my bloodstream when he came closer to me.

"Wanna tell me what's bothering you, all of a sudden?" I asked, peering at him.

He shrugged. "Me and P got into it, like always."

"It's funny how much older siblings act like they're our parents too."

"Man," he drawled. "Always worried about the wrong shit."

I laughed. "Having protective siblings isn't all it's cracked up to be, huh?"

"Not at all. When I need him to have my back, he's nowhere to be found," he groused while sitting on the couch. "I want to tell you what happened, but I don't want to scare you off."

My eyebrows met. "Me? The woman going through a divorce? I'm surprised you still want to talk to me."

Memphis smiled, making my insides tingle as I took a seat next to him.

"The woman in the last picture I showed is my ex. Paris thinks she used me in hopes of helping her father's business, but he's wrong. We broke up way before I lost my deal. And I was the reason it didn't work out, not her. Paris isn't hearing that though. This shit is so old, and I'm tired of rehashing it with him."

"Why does it bother him so much?"

"I guess because she's older than me. It's actually insulting for him to think I was preyed on. When I'm the one who approached her," he said with a chuckle. "What we had was real, and I wish I could share that with my brother. I'd always wanted love like him and Opal. What I had with Nalia was the closest I'd ever gotten to it."

"She was your first love, huh?" I asked him after a beat.

He looked at me cautiously, then said, "Yeah. I'm not in love with her anymore, though."

"No, I get it." I held up my hands. "Mark was my first love too. It takes some time to get over, but it stays with you. Our ending was a little more tragic than yours, so I had to let that love go sooner than I wanted."

Talking about our exes was easier than I imagined. I thought this would happen later down the line, but the timing was perfect.

"I didn't think we'd talk about exes so soon," Memphis said after a beat.

I smiled. "Neither did I. I'm glad we got it out the way, though. Our first date won't be awkward now."

"So, there is a first date?"

Heat flooded my cheeks. "Yes."

Hopefully.

Memphis reached into his pocket and pulled out his phone. "Maybe this time you'll leave your number."

Taking his phone from his hand, I replied, "I don't know why I didn't do it last time I was here."

He chuckled. "It didn't matter. I knew I was gonna see you again."

Memphis leaned closer, his lips hovering over mine. I tilted my head to the side, eager to taste him once more.

My phone chimed interrupting our almost kiss, and I groaned.

Alex: Don't make me miss my flight 'cause you want some mimosa dick!

I burst out laughing, making Memphis eyebrows wrinkle. I showed him the text and he laughed too.

"Your girl, Alex, is a trip."

"She is, but that's my bestie and I'ma stick beside her."

We left the guesthouse and joined everyone in the living room. Opal thanked me again for coming and promised to text me. Memphis walked us to the car and said bye to Alex first.

"I'll be back in a few months," she told him. "Take care of my girl."

Memphis looked at me. "I will."

Alex shrieked. "I like the sound of that!"

"Get in the car, silly," I told her, making Memphis laugh.

He hooked his arm around my waist, pulling me into him. "I'll hit you later this week."

"I look forward to it," I told him, then kissed his cheek.

Once we got home, I looked around my house for the perfect place to hand my butterfly, while Alex packed her bags. After walking through the living room, office, and my bedroom, I decided to hang it in my bathroom near my vanity.

Every day as I got ready, I wanted to be reminded that the changes in my life were the start of a new beginning.

CHAPTER SEVEN

Kiannah

This can't be good.

Suzanne stormed into the conference room with a manilla folder tucked under her arm. I expected champagne and croissants. Not a frustrated lawyer with a folder that more than likely contained *unsigned* documents.

"Kiannah, I have some bad news," she said, sitting down across from me. "Mark's lawyers can't get in contact with him."

My heart raced and eyes widened. "What do you mean they can't get in contact with him?"

"We've been trying to get him on the phone all week, to no avail. His lawyers think he's gotten cold feet."

Cold feet?

I knew this shit was too good to be true. While pinching the bridge of my nose, I sighed. "Okay, now what?"

"I know you didn't want to get the courts involved, but that may be our only option at this point."

"Going to court would only prolong the process. Didn't you say it could take up to a year if we went that route?"

Suzanne nodded. "Yes, but Mark hasn't been cooperative, and it's making it harder for all parties involved."

"His lawyers can't force him to sign? He's already agreed to do it."

"No, they can't."

"Why did he change his mind?"

"No one knows. They haven't heard from him since we last spoke. Normally, I wouldn't advise this but maybe you can get him on the phone? Sometimes the reluctant party is looking for closure."

Closure?

Mark didn't deserve any closure from me. Whatever answers he needed were from within. I wasn't the reason our marriage ended, and I damn sure wouldn't give him the satisfaction of apologizing for leaving his ass.

"I don't think I'm in a place to give him closure. Is there anything else that can be done?"

"Unfortunately, no," she said, with sad eyes.

"This is a lot to process."

Suzanne nodded. "I understand. Just think about it. I'll be in touch," she told me while sliding the folder across the table to me. "If you change your mind about seeing him, here's a copy of the documents. Maybe he'll sign them for you."

"Thanks," I mumbled as my mind raced.

Before leaving, Suzanne turned to me and said, "I like the haircut. It suits you."

I smiled while raking my fingers through my side bangs.

My smile disappeared once I was alone and had time to think. I was discouraging to hear Mark hadn't signed the papers. Not only that, but he was practically a ghost right now. I didn't want to speak to him without a neutral party involved. He was making this harder than it needed to be, and I was determined to stop him.

After leaving Suzanne's office, I sat outside of Maia's Sweet Treats, debating whether or not I wanted to go to his house. I killed the engine of my car and headed inside for a slice of coffee cake. My phone rang, stopping me in my tracks.

What does she want?

"Yes, Kym?" I answered the call while entering the bakery.

"You didn't come to dinner this week. We have so much food leftover." She paused. "I just wanted to check in with you is all."

As I waited to place my order, I looked at the desserts on display. Everything looked delicious.

"I'm good," I told Kym after a beat.

She hummed. "Everett told me about Mark and the baby…"

While palming my forehead, I pursed my lips together. "Yeah, I found out a few days ago. Haven't really processed it yet."

"Are you okay? I-I don't know what else to say.'"

Which is why I didn't want you to know yet.

"I'm fine, Kym. Hold on, I'm next in line." After placing my order, I stepped aside and waited for it to be warmed and bagged. "I'm okay, seriously. Have you told Mom yet?" I asked.

"No, I promise I won't. Me and Everett are staying out of it from now on."

"Okay," I said, unable to hide my laugh.

"Um, you and Mom need to talk soon. She's sorry for how she acted at the last dinner."

This time I didn't stifle my laugh. "Kym, I'll call her when I'm ready."

She sighed. "Come on, Kiannah."

"Flat white latte for Memphis!" the cashier said while holding up a coffee cup. I looked around the bakery, hoping to see him. Moments later, Memphis emerged from the corner of the room. I pressed on my toes to get a better look.

Yup, it's him.

Memphis grabbed the coffee, then returned to his seat. How did he get finer every time I saw him?

"Kym, I'll call you later," I told my sister, then ended our call. After grabbing my cake, I walked over to where he was seated. "Hey, you."

Memphis looked up from his laptop and smiled. *"You."*

The way he said the three-letter word made my insides melt. His deep, raspy drawl was intoxicating to say the least. Using his left leg, he pushed out the chair for me to sit.

"Sorry I haven't called," he started, but stopped once I held up my hand.

"You don't have to apologize to me." He nodded. "What are you working on?" I asked, looking at his laptop.

Memphis pushed out a deep breath, then turned his laptop screen to me.

"I'm working on a pitch for the Glacier National Park Museum. Lawrence and my agent, Loren, think it'll be a good project for me while I figure out my next book."

I clicked through the images, thoroughly impressed with what he'd taken so far.

"You took these this week?"

"Yeah, I've been walking the trails at the park and taking pictures here and there. Most of the photographs need editing, this is just a draft."

"I wouldn't know the difference," I said with a smile. "Have you ever done an exhibit before?"

Memphis nodded before drinking his latte. "I did in Chicago. My mentor was a curator at a museum and gave me a shot. It was a small showcase of five photographs. A little somethin' to get my feet wet."

"Ah, the pictures on your wall."

"You pay attention, I like that."

I bit my lip to conceal my smile. "Anyway," I crooned.

"Anyway, I promised to have this done by Monday. So, here I am bright and early on a Friday." He dropped his hands on his lap. "Where are you headed?" he asked, noting my business attire.

"I had a meeting with my divorce lawyer this morning."

He nodded. "How'd it go?"

"I don't want to get into it," I answered honestly.

My head hurt just from thinking about Mark. I needed to put my pride aside and reach out to him. Talking to him would take a lot of patience and prayer, but it had to happen. I couldn't allow him to prolong this anymore.

"All good. Let's talk about going to dinner tomorrow night, then?"

A smile formed on my lips. "Sounds good to me. Just text me the details." I stood from my seat, preparing to leave. "I don't want to distract you any longer."

"You're a good distraction though."

Shaking my head, I replied, "There's no such thing."

"It is. You'll see."

I rolled my eyes at him while butterflies swarmed my stomach. "I'll talk to you later."

Memphis grabbed my hand before I walked away, running hand thumb gently over my wrist.

"I'm happy we bumped into each other."

"Me too," I told him.

I wasn't upset that he hadn't called. He'd been here for a week and needed to get adjusted. It would've been silly for me to expect him to reach out so soon. However, I was happy to see him again. Something about Memphis's energy relaxed me.

"Are you gonna let go of my hand?" I asked.

"Do you want me to?"

Am I blushing, right now?

"I'm not answering that question."

He flashed a charming smile that had me second guessing if I should leave. Then, I remembered my to-do list for the day. Thanks to my dad, I had to make shirts for his entire bowling league. The remaining nine teams wanted custom shirts made pronto. I hadn't finished designing mockups for three teams, and it needed to be done by close of business today. Especially since I had a *date* tomorrow.

Memphis released my hand finally and went back to working on his pitch. When I got back to my car, I had a text from him with the details of our date night. After saving his number, and confirming the time, I went home.

MY STOMACH GROWLED JUST as I hit send on the last email of the day. I looked at the clock and thought back to the last meal I had.

Ah, that tuna sandwich from the deli.

I was ashamed when I realized hours had passed since I had last eaten. It was a Friday night and cooking was the last thing I wanted to do. However, I didn't feel like dealing with Main Street tonight. Everybody and their momma would be out tonight.

Kym has leftovers.

Did I really feel like dealing with her and Everett tonight, though? Looking around my workspace, I thought of an excuse to dip out early. I'd sent the mockups to each respective team captain and was waiting for a response. My dad said they were eager, so I expected to start working on shirts as early as tomorrow.

Yeah, that'll be my excuse.

I grabbed my jacket and hurried out the door en route to Kym's house. When I arrived, I was relieved to see that Everett's car wasn't in the driveway. But then, I got irritated when I remembered how close he and Mark were. Maybe he could talk some sense into his friend. I'd have to run it past Kym once I got inside.

"What are you doing here?" Kym asked when she opened the door.

My eyebrows wrinkled. "That's a different tune from earlier."

"I mean, I wasn't expecting you is all."

"Kym, I never give notice before coming over. What's wrong?"

She pulled me inside and locked the door. "Everett and Mark are on their way back from the bar."

"I only need five minutes to make a plate and leave."

Her eyes went wide when headlights beamed through their living room window.

"That's them."

I should've stayed my ass at home.

"I'll come by another time," I rushed out then stormed out the door. Mark noticed my car and jumped out, stopping me in my tracks.

"Kiannah, baby."

Shaking my head, I said, "Don't start, Mark."

Heat coursed my veins from the sad-puppy dog eyes he had while staring at me. He reeked of alcohol, his hair hadn't been cut in I didn't know how long, and his five o'clock shadow was damn near six.

"I-I wanted to see you," he slurred while leaning against Everett's car.

Everett came around to the passenger's side and said, "Key, hey. I, uh… stopped him from going to your house."

"Our… it's our house," Mark corrected, making me roll my eyes. "It's our house, baby."

He reached for my hand, and I snatched it away. "Eww, Mark. You smell like alcohol. How much did he drink?"

Everett shrugged. "He was a few shots in by the time I got there."

"Listen, baby. I-I'm glad you're here." Mark tried to stand but stumbled back onto Everett's car. "We need to talk."

I glanced over my shoulder at the manilla folder on my back seat. "Yeah, we do. Everett, can you give us a minute?"

"Are you sure?" he asked. We looked at Mark who was holding his head.

I nodded. "Yeah, it won't take long."

Everett went inside, while Kym remained in the doorway. I wasn't worried about being alone with Mark. He wasn't violent, just a womanizer. Besides, he was too inebriated to try anything.

"Why are you making this so hard?" I asked Mark.

His gloss covered eyes met mine. "You really done with me? After all these years, man. After all we've been through."

"Yes." I folded my arms over my chest. "I'm really done with you, Mark. I can't believe this is even a question. You have a child with someone else."

He nodded his head. "I didn't mean for it to happen, and I wish it hadn't."

"Well, it's too late for that now, huh." I slid my hand into my jacket pocket and pressed the button on my key fob. Once the doors unlocked, I grabbed the folder from the backseat. "It's over, Mark. Sign the papers and let's go our separate ways, peacefully."

Mark took the folder and held it at his side. "I'm sorry for hurting you, Kiannah. For real. You were the only family I had, and I fucked that up."

I looked at Kym and Everett's house while pushing out a deep breath.

"They're your family too. You're not alone out here." I held his hand, then said, "And maybe it's time you reach out to your parents. It's been years since you called."

Before our breakup, we discussed him reconnecting with his parents.

When we moved here, they graciously gave him their cabin and I thought it would've opened the door to them talking again. After a year passed, I learned this wasn't an overnight fix. Mark kept a brave face, but I knew the distance was weighing on him.

He nodded. "Yeah, I will."

We stood in an awkward silence for a few seconds. I gave Mark time to gather himself before calling Everett to get him. With his arm thrown over Everett's shoulder, Mark smiled at me.

"You cut your hair? Yeah, you wasn't taking my ass back."

Me and Everett laughed because it was true.

I was happy our conversation ended on a good note. Before parting ways, I made sure Everett knew Mark needed to review the documents the moment he sobered up. He promised me everything would be fine as they trekked up the walkway. Once they made it safely to the door, I got started backing out of the driveway. Kym ran out the door with two bags in her hand, reminding me the reason I stopped by in the first place.

"I made you enough plates to last through the weekend." She handed me the bags. "Call me when you get home."

I nodded, then resumed backing out of the driveway.

Finally.

Mark and I were done, finally and legally.

My eyes watered from the realization.

Soon, I'd have to think about my next steps. After meeting with a realtor earlier this week, I was reconsidering selling the house. I was uninterested in the whole process. Plus, the house was becoming mine. I'd thrown out all the ugly furniture Mark purchased. The home was warm, inviting, and represented me. I'd never had my own place before. I went from having two roommates in college to living with Mark. The idea of living alone was as exciting as getting a new haircut... or going on a date with a guy I was actually into.

I beamed thinking about my upcoming date with Memphis. If our date was anything like today at the bakery, I looked forward to it. Those few minutes we spent catching up changed my day. I wasn't sure what my intentions with him were, but I was enjoying the ride. I appreciated that there wasn't any pressure–on either side–to move at a certain pace, we just vibe. Maybe we were so in sync because we were both in a transitional space. We understood the importance of inching into something new.

Whatever the reason, I was grateful for our budding friendship.

And maybe, one day it would be something more.

CHAPTER EIGHT

Memphis

I was walking along a trail, taking pictures when my phone rang. Loren only called early in the morning when she had good news. I braced myself for the worst though because that's what I'd grown accustomed to hearing lately.

"Memphis! I just got off the phone with Isaac Preston, an editor at Topaz Media. I sent him a copy of your book, and he loved it."

After pushing out a breath, I said, "That's wassup. What else did y'all talk about?"

"Having them possibly publish your next book. I know you're working on something else right now, but Isaac seemed interested."

"You think I can do both?"

Because I didn't think I could. I was still feeling a little insecure about my art and didn't want to put too much pressure on myself.

"No, the exhibit, if it happens, would come first. I was just seeing if you're ready to start the publishing process."

It had only been a week since I moved to Hidden Lake. I was in no way ready to restart the publishing process. The mere thought of negotiating a deal made my head hurt.

My silence must've unnerved Loren because she swiftly changed the topic.

"You finish the pitch?"

I nodded. "Yeah, I think I'm done."

"Don't overthink it, Memphis. You got this."

I can't help but overthink.

"You think Topaz Media is a good look?" I asked after a moment. They were a smaller publisher, which meant a more personalized experience. It also meant less money.

"Yes! I think you and Isaac would work well together, which is why I reached out to him. This isn't the same situation as before," Loren said, sensing my apprehension.

"I hear you."

"Enjoy your weekend, and if you need me to look over your pitch, I'm available."

"Thanks Loren."

Just as I ended the call, I reached a bluff with a view of the upcoming sunrise. I checked the time, and I had a few minutes before the sun peered over Heaven's Peak. I'd been trying to get the perfect angle for days, but always missed it. I changed the lens and quickly got into position.

Heaven's peak was beautiful. The mix of pinks and purples behind the peak made the scene ethereal-like. After capturing a few different angles, I waited for the sun to rise just above the peak.

I smiled, happy to be back in my element. Even though I was still a little uneasy about my pitch, I had to admit, it felt good working again. The Glacier National Park Museum had never done a photo series on the mountains in the area. Before Isaac, the curators were only interested in having artifacts, paintings, and fossils exhibits. My photos would bring something new to the museum.

No pressure.

Lawrence made the opportunity sound like I wasn't being overly ambitious with my pitch. Could my photographs be as poignant and revered as the relics and articles they'll neighbor?

Again, no pressure.

I shook away those thoughts and continued along the trail. After checking the time on my phone, I decided to head back to my car. If I wanted to finish the pitch today, I'd need to spend most of the day editing. I didn't want anything to distract me while I was with Kiannah.

This pitch had taken over my life. I felt terrible for not calling her this week. My lack of contact could've been perceived as inconsistent or disinterested. Two words I'd been called more than I cared to admit. I chuckled when I thought about how she cut off my apology. It was refreshing to receive grace.

Once I got home, I spent several hours sorting through and editing the footage from this morning. By the time I finished, I didn't have long to wait for my night with Kiannah. I wanted to skip the awkward first date dinner, so I planned a date that appealed to our creative sides.

I was doing all I could to ignore the fact that this was the first real date I'd been on in months. I reminded myself not to be too serious. First dates often felt like interviews with invasive questions and trying to avoid showing too many flaws too soon. It was my least favorite part of meeting someone new. Kiannah and I kind of bypassed the awkward parts already. She was up front about her relationship status, and I'd told her about my ex. For me, that was the most challenging part of a new relationship.

Is this the start of a relationship, though?

I needed to slow down. Things were cool right now. The moment I started overthinking, shit would get complicated.

After getting dressed, I went to my brother's house to look for Opal, who insisted that I borrow her car tonight. I wanted to rent one for the weekend because the thought of having to borrow my sister-in-law's car seemed lame. She didn't want to hear that, though.

Just as I suspected, she was in the kitchen opening a bottle of wine.

"Long day?"

Opal groaned. "Yes. I've got to stop agreeing to work on Saturday's. It's never worth it."

"Where's P?" I asked, grabbing the keys of the counter.

"Probably at the club." Her eyes narrowed, and head tilted to the side. "I thought y'all kissed and made up?"

I chuckled before replying, "We're cool. I just hadn't really seen him in a few days."

There was some tension between us after the argument at brunch, but I nipped it in the bud later that night. I did something I never thought I was capable of doing, being vulnerable with my big brother. We surprised each other that night. He finally articulated why he hated Nalia so much. She broke my heart; it was plain and simple. Apparently, I wasn't the same after the breakup and he noticed it. He was more frustrated that he couldn't do anything to make me feel better. I reiterated it was something I had to deal with on my own.

However, I wasn't innocent. The moment I realized I was in love, I shut down. I'd go days without calling, and when she'd confront me about it, I turned it on her. Nalia gave me chance after chance to open my heart. She recognized I wasn't ready to be all in and didn't hold it against me. We remained friends and continued to work together. In hindsight, it probably made the breakup harder for me, but it forced me to grow up.

Opal's stare snapped me out of my thoughts. "You okay?"

I nodded. "Yeah, I'm cool."

"Aw, you have first date jitters."

My eyebrows furrowed as I said, "Nah."

Opal smiled, then said, "Have fun tonight," before leaving the kitchen.

Shortly after, I left to pick up Kiannah.

KIANNAH'S EYES widened when she realized where I was taking her. When her lips curved into a smile, I knew I'd made the right choice.

"Sip and Paint?" she beamed as we entered Cork & Easel, a painting studio located on Main Street.

"Yeah. Sound good?"

Kiannah giggled. "Yes, I love this place."

We entered the studio and checked in at the front

desk.

"You know what you want to paint?" Kianna asked then pointed at the display case containing glasses, canvases, ceramic bowls and vases.

"A canvas?" I replied with a wrinkled brow.

"You sure?"

"Okay, let's do the bowls," I suggested.

"I think that's best. I don't know about you, but I am not that good of a painter." She giggled while raking her fingers through her side bangs. The innocent gesture made my chest tighten.

"You like to paint?" I asked once we were situated at our station.

Kiannah laughed. "A little. Alex and I try to come here when she's in town. We only paint wine glasses and vases. It's easier to finish when you've had a few drinks."

Alex was the one who suggested this place. I got her number from Opal and hit her up about date ideas earlier in the week. I made the reservation here at the last minute, luckily, they had a slot available.

"We should paint a bowl for each other," Kiannah said. "I think that'll be cute."

I smirked. "What colors do you want me to use for your bowl?"

She looked at the selection of paint in the bin beside her. A beat passed before she handed me the colors blue and fuchsia. I searched through the bin and handed her black and silver. Kiannah rolled her eyes at the color's I'd selected.

"Typical."

"I'm a simple man."

Her eyes roved over me and stopped once they met mine. I waited for her to say something slick, but instead she picked up her wine glass. Our host returned and gave us directions on how to paint the bowls. After a brief tutorial, we placed the bowls upside down, and started painting.

While working on our bowls, we talked about our week. Kiannah had a rush of orders after her dad's bowling match that kept her busy during the week. She lightly touched on the meeting she had with her lawyer, which led to her talking about her family's lack of support.

"I haven't had the best support from my family throughout this process. I mean, my sister tries to be supportive, but..." she shrugged.

"They must've really liked him," I noted.

I didn't want to ask questions, and risk saying the wrong thing. Family and divorce were delicate topics.

Kiannah nodded, her attention on the bowl as she painted. "Yeah. Everyone loves him. It makes me wonder how they'll act when I remarry."

"You'd get married again?"

"Absolutely. I'm not jaded. I still have hope that the one is out there." Kiannah stopped painting and looked at me. "You want to fall in love again? Or are you too afraid of being heartbroken?"

I chuckled. "I'm willing to fall again. This time I won't be afraid of it, though."

Kiannah giggle, making me smile. "You were wide open, huh?"

"Wide open doesn't even begin to explain it."

"I liked that feeling. When you first fall, it's like a high. And I chased that high for as long as I could; it didn't last very long," she told me. "But let's talk about something else. We have a tendency to get deep."

We laughed because it was true. I hadn't been this open with anyone this soon. I guess it was another reminder of how comfortable we were with each other. The thought should've scared me, but I welcomed it.

"How did you get into print design?"

"I wanted a career in fashion, but I took the safe route and went to school for social work." Her smirk had me wondering why she didn't follow through her original plans. "My parents, specifically my mom, wanted me to have a real career. They paid for my education, so I did it."

"Social work. That's an intense field."

"Right? My internship during senior year was enough to scare me away. I worked temp jobs until I moved back home. Then, I worked with my dad for a bit, which was an experience." Kiannah laughed while shaking her head. "Working with him was the last straw. It's been up ever since."

Kiannah stared at me while grinning. I stopped paining and gazed her way, catching the desire in her eyes.

Don't look at me like that.

"Wassup?" I asked and resumed painting.

She didn't answer, instead she sipped her wine and continued to paint. A few minutes passed before I realized I zoned out. Kiannah's sighs caught my attention as she sat back in her chair.

"I don't think the line isn't thick enough," she mused.

Rotating the bowl on the table, Kiannah examined the silver stripe.

"It's fine," I assured her. "Besides, it's time for the next activity."

"In that case," she sang and began cleaning her space.

While we cleaned up, the host brought out two flights of wine, and a small charcuterie board. Alex mentioned how much Kiannah enjoyed their boards, so I had to get one too. I waited until after we finished painting. We ate the cheese and ham while Kiannah told me about the first date she went on after separating from her husband.

"Do I look like I want to go paintballing?" Kiannah covered her mouth to muffle her chortles.

"In his defense, y'all met at the gym."

"And I have been back since. I had bruises on my thighs for weeks." Kiannah pulled her dress up her thigh and pointed at a small mark. "This is from paintballing," she told me while pouting.

"Aw. You want me to kiss it?" I teased while rubbing the faded mark with my thumb.

Her eyes lowered. "Yes."

I grinned then leaned down to her thigh. Before my lips could touch her, she pushed me back.

"You play too much."

"I'm not playin'."

Kiannah licked her lips before saying, "We'll see soon, won't we?"

I scooted my chair closer to hers, invading her space. She sighed when I placed my hand on her thigh, trailing my fingers in between her legs.

"Yeah, we will," I said, then kissed her.

CHAPTER NINE

Kiannah

I knew he wasn't playing.

My breaths quickened as Memphis dropped warm, sweet kisses along my inner thigh. I held the back of the couch for support when he spread my legs wider. Poor couch. It was brand new and would soon be ruined thanks to Memphis.

Fuck this couch.

Memphis hiked my dress over my hips and slid my panties aside. His adroit fingers parted my lips, and his tongue landed on my clit. My back arched, and whimpers fell from my lips. I grabbed his hands and guided them under my dress. His big hands caressed my sides and roved up my stomach to my taut nipples. He tweaked them, applying just the right amount of pressure to make me moan.

I knew Memphis wouldn't disappoint. The energy he had when he kissed me, deeply and with fervor, was the same way he treated my clit. His mouth was busy, kissing and licking my pussy while I moved my hips. I held his shoulders as my stomach tightened, bracing myself for an intense orgasm. Memphis held my thighs tighter and continued thrashing my clit with his tongue. He didn't stop after the first one.

"I told you I wasn't playing," he crooned. I giggled, then bit my bottom lip. He damn sure wasn't playing with me.

Using his thumb, he massaged my clit while peering at me. I watched a slow smirk form on his lips. I shot him a smirk of my own, feeling light-headed from my last climax. He kissed me ardently and slid two fingers into my wetness. I ended our kiss, unable to hold back my moans as another orgasm overcame me.

"That's it, huh?" he taunted, making me wetter. Memphis hoarse chords sent chills down my spine. "Answer me."

"Mhm. Yes," I hummed. Memphis chuckled throatily as my wetness covered his hand.

I'm so glad I bought condoms earlier.

I didn't think I'd need them tonight, but I wasn't complaining. Memphis followed me upstairs to my room. On the dresser, still in the pharmacy bag were the box of condoms I'd purchased. Memphis did the honors of opening the box and sheathing himself. I waited in bed, my body humming for him. Once he was in bed, I straddled him and slid on his dick.

We groaned, our bodies immediately collided as I rolled my hips. Memphis's arms held me close while he pumped into me. I angled my head, welcoming his lips on my neck. Each kiss sent a jolt of electricity through me. My hips jerked as I lost my once steady rhythm.

Memphis laid back, pulling me with him. I moaned in his mouth while moving my hips slowly. He gripped my waist and pumped into me. It was no use in trying to control the flow. My body wasn't my own right now. Memphis had seized control with his strong hold, ardent kisses, and steady stroke. I stopped kissing him long enough to cry in pleasure as an orgasm ripped through me.

He chuckled menacingly against the shell of my ear. It was so sexy. My stomach muscles tightened as I fought to catch my breath. Memphis didn't care that I could hardly breathe, he kissed me anyway. Brushing his lips against mine while smiling, he then sucked my bottom lip.

"You want me to kiss it?" he asked, reminding me of how we got here in the first place. He pushed into me then slowly pulled out.

I let out a sound that was a mix between a giggle and a moan.

"Yes."

Our lips met for a slow, lazy kiss. His raspy moans made my pussy throb as he reached his peak.

A beat passed before I spoke. "You want to stay the night?"

Memphis chuckled and pulled me next to him. "I was hoping you'd ask."

Snuggling under him, I fell asleep feeling desired and protected.

"YOU HUNGRY?"

I'd barely wiped the crust from my eyes when Memphis spoke.

"How long have you been awake?"

"Not long. I was looking over the notes Lawrence sent about my pitch. There aren't many changes to make."

Sitting up, I asked, "You nervous?"

"Very," he told me with the cutest grin. "I need to make some adjustments, but don't try to change the subject. You hungry? I could go for something sweet."

"First thing in the morning?"

Memphis laughed. "Man, Maia's Sweet Treats got me in a chokehold."

"Her coffee cake is addicting. I'll take two and a toasted white latte."

He nodded, then started getting dressed.

"Can you open the curtains?" I asked while checking my text messages.

Alex was eager to hear about my date last night. I promised to call her afterward, little did she know, the date wasn't over.

"You expecting company?" Memphis asked, peeking through the blinds.

"No!"

Before he could respond, I hurried over to the window.

"Stay here until I come back," I told him, then grabbed a shirt and pair of shorts from my dresser.

The doorbell rang just as I hit the bottom step. After attempting to fix my hair, I opened the door.

"Ma, what are you doing here?"

"When did you change the locks and the code to the garage?"

I pushed out a breath. "A while ago."

Ten months to be exact.

But she wouldn't have known because she refused to come over after I kicked Mark out. I was glad I hadn't bothered giving her a key. And the code to the garage was updated too, or else she would've known I had company.

"Are you alone? Is Dad okay?"

She rolled her eyes, and looked down at the flowers on my doorstep. My eyebrows met as I leaned down to retrieve them. Only one man knew how much I adored orchids. I pulled out the card and read it with a smile.

It's done.
-Mark

"Already have a new boyfriend, huh?" she asked, brushing by me to come inside.

While holding up the card, I replied, "Actually, they're from Mark."

"It's done? What does that mean?"

I nodded, still smiling. "He's gonna stop fighting me."

"You mean fighting *for* you."

It's too early for this.

"So, you were just in the neighborhood and decided to stop by?" I asked.

It was unlike her to pop up like this, especially since we lived on opposite sides of Hidden Lake. When Mark and I toured the neighborhood, I was bummed about the distance. However, I was grateful for space now.

My mother continued to the kitchen and sat at the island. "It's been three weeks."

She looked at everything meticulously. I already knew she was looking for something to critique. The house looked nothing like it did last year; just as I intended.

"I hadn't noticed," I replied.

I folded my arms over my chest. She shouldn't have popped up like this. A simple phone call would've worked. I couldn't tell if she was ready to talk or if this was another battle in our never-ending war.

"Kiannah," she warned. "Your sister seems to think I'm being too hard on you about this divorce thing. But I really just don't understand what he could've done for you to leave him. Mark loves you, baby."

"And I loved him, but he cheated on me... a lot."

She gasped. "What?"

"Yup and this last time he got someone pregnant, so," I told her while shrugging. "He had to go."

I pushed out a breath. It felt good to finally tell her the truth. However, the mortified expression she had saddened me.

"A baby?" she questioned, gazing at me with teary eyes. Her emotional response evoked feelings I thought were buried.

A sneaky tear fell from my eye, and I swiftly wiped it away.

I wanted a baby.

Mark took the excitement I had about becoming parents without blinking an eye. I'd expressed my desire to be a mother just a few months before he broke the news. We'd just moved into this house, he got the promotion he worked so hard for, and my business was thriving. It only made sense to have a child next.

While I was happy it didn't happen, it still stung.

My mom pulled me into a loving embrace. The tears I held back fell in rapid succession.

"I'm so sorry, baby," my mom said, rocking me back and forth. "I'm sorry this happened."

I savored my mom's comfort. Her comfort was all I needed during this journey. She released me to grab a paper towel. I used it to dab away the tears on my cheeks.

She cupped my face, forcing me to meet her gaze. "I'm sorry for not being there for you, baby. You hear me."

I nodded as another wave of tears fell. "I'm sorry for being so guarded the past year."

My mom shook her head. "This is my fault," she said, dropping her head. "I pushed you to marry him when you clearly weren't ready."

My eyebrows shot up.

I hadn't expected her to admit what I'd been repressing all along. When Mark proposed, I wasn't ready for marriage. I was at a crossroads in my life and committing the rest of my life to him was a big ask. The first time he asked, I didn't immediately answer. After a week, Mark called my mom and she shamed me into accepting his proposal.

According to her, I should've been jumping at the chance to marry him. If we broke up, I wouldn't find another man willing to love and support me like he had. It was the worst thing to hear during the most uncertain point of my life. Several days after our conversation, he proposed again, and I said, "Yes."

I pushed for a long engagement, but Mark was against it. Eventually, I grew tired of fighting it, so we got married.

"I should've left sooner," I said after a moment. "But it's over now and I've learned my fair share of lessons."

My mom was silent. I figured she was processing everything we discussed.

"You know, I still talk to Mark weekly. He never mentioned the baby, ever."

"He was somewhat in denial, and ashamed."

She pulled out her phone. "I'm gonna block him. I never want to talk to him again."

"Ma, stop." A sigh fell from my lips.

I can't believe I'm about to say this.

"I'm giving him permission to stay in contact with y'all."

Her eyebrows furrowed. "You sure?"

"Yes. It won't be easy, and I don't want to know when you see him or talk to him. But I know how close he is to everyone."

"Joe is gonna be so disappointed when he hears this."

I nodded as I pictured Dad's reaction. He might be the only one who'd cut him off. If it was one thing he hated, it was a cheater. Another reason why I was hesitant to tell my parents. I wasn't sure how my dad would handle the news.

"I'm sure he'll call with questions and comments."

My mom laughed. "That's for sure. He'll have his pen and pad ready to take notes. Be prepared to be smothered."

I rolled my eyes. "I'm already annoyed."

We fell silent. I was glad my mom came over and we got this conversation out the way. We had a long way to go before things were good between us, but this was a step.

"Thanks for coming over," I told her. She patted my arm, then prepared to leave.

"See, being aggressive isn't always a bad thing."

"Anyway," I droned.

After walking her to the front door we shared another embrace. My mom raked her fingers through side bangs. Her eyes narrowed and mouth twisted.

"This haircut is growing on me."

A smile formed on my lips because I knew that was her way of complimenting me.

"Thanks, Ma," I told her before we parted ways.

Once her car was down the street, I sighed. I sat on the couch and sorted through my thoughts. My family finally knew the truth. I heard footsteps padding down the stairs, and ran my hands over my face. Hopefully, Memphis hadn't heard our conversation. I waited for him to come to the living room to gauge his energy.

"You good?" he asked with furrowed eyebrows.

Flashing a half-smile, I replied, "Yup."

"Cool. I'll be back with the food." He dropped a chaste kiss on my forehead.

I nodded as he left, hoping my mom's surprise visit wouldn't change things. The last thing I needed was for my family drama to push him away.

CHAPTER TEN

Memphis

I wiped my eyes, making sure I wasn't imagining the words on the screen.

Closing my laptop, I pushed out a breath, then smiled. Lawrence and his colleagues wanted *my* photographs in their museum.

Let's go!

My chest felt like it was about to burst.

This shit was surreal.

I reopened my laptop and read the email again. My eyes widened as I read the details of my future exhibit. An opening in the spring, interviews, and the opportunity to work with other National Park museums in the future; I didn't need time to consider accepting. I'd be a fool not to do it.

I responded to the email and accepted their offer, before sharing the news with my family. Opal and Paris were cleaning their house to prepare for our parents' arrival. I didn't realize how seriously my family took the holiday's until I saw Opal's menu. In the past, I spent the holiday in whatever country I resided at the time.

"O!" I yelled from the bottom of the stairs. She appeared moments later frowning. "The museum wants me to do the exhibit," I told her.

She descended the steps and hugged me. "That's great! I knew they'd love your pictures. Paris went to the store for me, but he should be back soon."

"Yeah, I want to tell him before telling our parents."

"Better do it soon. They'll be here in a few hours."

"Why are they coming so early? Thanksgiving isn't for another week."

Opal shrugged. "I think your parents just like being here. We're trying to convince them to move here and be done with it."

I had no idea they liked Hidden Lake.

The somewhat small town was charming and was the perfect home for two retirees. The more I explored Hidden Lake, the more I liked it too. I finally explored the town beyond its trails and the views. The architecture and design on Main Street recently caught my eye. The night before my pitch, I took pictures of the town's crown jewel. I think those pictures added character to the presentation. Not many people knew Hidden Lake was located in the heart of those peaks and mountains.

"What are you doing upstairs anyway?" I asked her.

"Preparing the rooms for our parents. I've been procrastinating all week."

I pushed out a breath while shaking my head. "How do you do it every year?"

Opal's parents plus me and Paris's parents were a combination. Our dads were outspoken, and stubborn, which made dinner's interesting.

"When they start debating, everyone goes their separate ways. Don't chime in, ever."

While nodding, I replied, "Got it."

I went back to the guest house and grabbed my phone. There was one other person I wanted to share the news with, Kiannah. The days leading up to my presentation, we didn't talk much. Admittedly, I was nervous, and needed space to prepare. I was just as anxious as anxious the night before my book released.

"You busy?" I asked when she answered.

"Nope. I'm on my way to the Post Office to drop off some packages."

"When you're done, stop by."

"Why? You miss me?"

I smirked. "I do. You've been ducking me all week."

Kiannah giggled. "I promise, I haven't."

"Prove it then," I taunted her.

"I'll be there soon."

Half an hour later, Kiannah arrived, and Paris was right behind her. I helped him unload the car while Kiannah talked to Opal.

"I got some good news, man," I told him, unable to contain my smile.

His eyebrows met. "What?"

"I'm doing the exhibit."

Paris smiled. "Congrats. We get to keep you a few more months, huh?"

Running my hand over my head, I replied, "Yeah, I'll be here for a bit."

The idea of staying until the spring didn't seem so bad. Once the exhibit was finished, I'd know for sure if I want to stay.

"Wassup with you and Kiannah?" Paris asked as we carried the bags inside.

I shrugged. "I don't know, but I do know that I like her, and I wanna see where this could go."

There was no point in downplaying my feelings for her.

Paris nodded. "You ask her about the divorce?"

"No. As far as I know, it's still happening." Paris glanced at me, his expression wary. "You don't need to worry about that," I told him.

We placed the bags in the kitchen, then joined the ladies in the living room. Opal was showing Kiannah pictures of the place settings she bought for Thanksgiving.

"You and my sister should meet," Kiannah told Opal. "She loves stuff like this. I'm supposed to be helping her prepare for a pre-Thanksgiving meal tonight."

"Wait, she cooks a big meal the week before?"

Kiannah giggled, making my chest tighten. "Yes. She's a mess."

"Opal, that's something you would do, if you had the time," Paris chimed in, and Opal nodded.

"Kiannah," I said her name, then pointed my head toward the door. "O, let me know if you need help with anything," I told Opal.

She waved her hand, politely declining my offer. "I'm

good. Paris, you need to be on your way to the airport. You know your parents hate waiting."

"Yeah, don't be late like you were with me," I chided.

"And Memphis, remember we have reservations at seven." Opal's eyebrow rose and her gaze bounced between me and Kiannah.

I chuckled at her subtle reminder, then took Kiannah by the hand. Once we were in the guest house, I pinned her to the door and kissed her. She smiled against my lips while grabbing the hem of my shirt.

"Now, do you believe me?" I asked, then kissed her neck.

She nodded. "Yes."

Kiannah released my shirt and cupped my face. "I have something to tell you, but I don't know how it'll sound."

"Just say it."

"When my mom stopped by, I was so embarrassed and afraid that you might've overheard our conversation."

My eyebrows furrowed. "I didn't hear anything," I assured her, but it made me wonder what they talked about.

She didn't sound convinced. "Are you sure?"

"Positive. Why were you talking about me or something?" I tried to lighten the mood.

Kiannah shook her head, then bit her bottom lip. She slid past me walked over to the couch.

"We had a fight and needed to talk. I also needed to tell her the truth about why I filed for divorce."

I joined her on the couch. "You thought I would care if I overheard that? I don't care why you left, I'm just happy you did."

"Because the whole situation is embarrassing. It's a long story."

"You don't have to tell me if you aren't ready, baby."

She nodded. "I just wanted admit that you were right. I was avoiding you."

"Look, I know your last relationship was hard, and you're still healing from it. You don't have to worry about me judging you, that's not my thing."

"Thank you for being so understanding, Memphis. I never thought I'd meet a man so accepting of my current situation."

Kiannah leaned in planted the sweetest kiss on cheek.

"Man, if there is anyone who recognizes the importance of patience and understanding, it's me. And the fact that I like you more than I probably should…" I added, feeling a little anxious about sharing my feelings with her.

Her eyes lowered, and her lips curved into a smile.

"I like you too," she replied, and my heart thudded against my chest.

"Good, 'cause I gonna be here for a while. Lawrence and his colleagues want me to do the exhibit."

Kiannah's eyes widened as she threw her arms around my neck. "Really? Congrats!" she hugged me tightly, making heat course my veins. "So, what happens next?"

"Next, I want to do some research on Hidden Lake, explore the town's gems, and learn more about the community."

"I can help with that," she said. "If you need me to."

The gleam of interest in her eyes had me thinking

about something else. Interest turned into lust when I placed my hand on her thigh. "I'd like that."

Kiannah's phone rang, making her shift to retrieve her phone from her back pocket.

She rolled her eyes, playfully then answered, "Hey, Kymmie. I'll be there in ten."

After ending the call, she stood up. "I have to go, but we should grab a drink to celebrate. Maybe this weekend?"

As much as I wanted to celebrate, and spend more time with her, I had family plans this weekend. It was too soon for her to meet them, and I didn't want either of us to feel pressured.

"I'm sure I'll need a drink after my parents get here," I said, walking her to the door.

She laughed, then kissed me once more. "If you want or need an escape, I'm here."

In response, I captured her lips with mine. Her offer was one I couldn't refuse. We kissed with fervor, the taste of her lips, igniting a fire neither of us had time to address. Reluctantly, she pulled away, and sighed.

"I have to go."

You need to go before I take you down, right here.

"Yeah," I cut her off, sighing.

"I meant what I said about being here if you need to hide out."

I dropped a chaste kiss on her forehead. "Come on. Let me walk you to your car before I convince you to stay."

I WISH I could say I was happy to see my parents. Well, I was happy to see my mom. She couldn't wait to hear about what I'd been doing since I landed. My dad on the other hand, he was ready to criticize every decision I'd made thus far. As we sat down at a five-star restaurant Paris selected, I couldn't help but feel uneasy. Aside from the fact that I was the fifth wheel, the tension between me and my dad was stifling.

Everyone felt it too.

"How are you liking Hidden Lake," my mom asked me after everyone ordered their drinks.

With a shrug, I replied, "It's cool. It's slower than what I'm used to, but I'm getting adjusted."

Opal kissed her teeth. "He's well-adjusted actually." She nodded, urging me to continue.

"Paris introduced me to Lawrence who is a curator at the Glacier National Park Museum, and we met earlier this week to discuss me doing an exhibit."

My dad's eyebrows rose, and he shifted in his seat. "Really?"

It was the first time he spoke to me all night.

Glancing his way, I nodded. "Yup. I showed them some of my work and they loved it. I'm gonna start working on the series soon."

My dad looked at Paris, then back to me, and nodded. "When's the opening?"

"Sometime this spring," I told him. "When I get the dates, I'll let you know."

"We'll be here," mom said, oozing with pride. "Hopefully, you'll find a reason to stay here and settle down too."

Paris chuckled. "You don't have to worry about that, Mom. He's already working on it."

I shot him a look that made him chuckle. It was too soon to tell my parents about Kiannah. if I hadn't met her at his bar, he wouldn't know about her either.

The waiter came and took our orders, but my mom picked up right where Paris left off.

"You met someone, already?" my mom asked me, grinning. "One step closer to finding my future daughter-in-law."

I knew she was serious, but I couldn't hold back my laughter. I blamed Paris for getting married in his twenties. Now, my mom thought I was behind because I hadn't gotten married yet. I hadn't even gotten thought about proposing before.

"She's just a friend," I said, downplaying the connection I had with Kiannah. "I haven't been here long enough for it to be anything serious."

She nodded. "Uh huh."

"Seriously. I just met her."

Here I was over explaining myself to mask how nervous her question made me. She grabbed my hand and tugged it.

"You don't have to lie, baby," she leaned closer, so only I could hear. "I can tell you really like this… friend. We'll talk later."

While shaking my head, I picked up my old fashion and took a gulp.

My dad peered around my mom to meet my gaze. "You're done with the publishing thing, huh?"

I knew this was coming.

"Actually, no. Loren is working on a deal with another publishing company. I'm gonna focus on this exhibit first, though."

"So, you do have a plan?" he sneered.

"Always," I shot back, feeling defensive. Paris and I exchanged a look that made him change the subject.

Paris talked about the success of The Oak Bar and how he was ready for his next business venture, a restaurant. Our dad immediately perked up and offered to help. I wish I wasn't bothered by his excitement when it came to Paris, but I brushed it off. My mom switched gears to grandchildren which made everyone laugh.

"We'll pack up and move here when you have my grand-babies."

Opal laughed. "I'ma hold you to that."

"You too," my mom said to me.

"That won't be happening anytime soon," I told her, making her sigh.

"Anyway," Paris droned, tired of talking about children. It was no secret that he wasn't ready for fatherhood. He was too focused on running the bar and expanding. I didn't know how Opal felt about it though. it wasn't *my* business, really.

While everyone talked, I pulled out my phone and texted Kiannah.

Me: Does the offer still stand?

Kiannah answered almost immediately, making me smile.

Kiannah: Of course.

Me: I'll call you when I'm on the way.

I put my phone away and joined the conversation.

Knowing I'd see her later made dinner a little more palatable. I ignored my dad's smart remarks and reminded myself that this was temporary.

After Thanksgiving and Christmas, I wouldn't have to deal with his antics for a while.

CHAPTER ELEVEN

Kiannah

I glanced around the kitchen at my mom and sister who were cooking. Kym handed me a bowl of string beans, and I sat down and started snapping them. It had been a while since we all cooked together. Last year, I didn't help cook because I was depressed about my separation to get in the holiday spirit. There was a different energy in the air this year.

My mom was in a great mood tonight.

I wasn't sure if our conversation had anything do with it, but it was nice to be on the receiving end of her kindness. Since that day, we were back to speaking regularly. We talked more about me and less about Mark and the divorce. I knew our relationship wouldn't ever be perfect, but it was somewhat back to normal.

Kym looked at me with a hiked brow. I was too busy snapping beans to realize Mom was talking to me.

"What did you say?" I asked, looking at my mom.

She rolled her eyes. "I asked if you had heard from your lawyer?"

Kym's eyes were fixed on me.

"Yes. All I have to do now is wait for it to be finalized. So, sometime after the holidays," I beamed.

My mom nodded while Kym smiled.

I knew their reactions were from a place of happiness. I waited to tell them because I wanted to enjoy the moment first. Kym and my mom had strong opinions—good and bad—about the divorce. I needed to appreciate the moment without bias.

"So… now what?" Kym asked.

Here we go.

I shrugged. "I don't know."

There was an uncomfortable silence. My mom and Kym exchanging a look that made me like the third wheel; like always.

"The house looked nice," my mom said after a moment. "You like living alone?"

Don't ask about the house.

My mom had complimented my house countless times this week. It was hard to determine if she really liked or if she was trying to get me to open up. Either way, I was over it.

"I do."

"You still working with that realtor?"

I glared at Kym, who actively ignored me. I hadn't forgotten that she told Mom. Lucky for her, this conversation was civil.

"No. I'm not interested in selling right now," I told my mom.

My mom smiled. "Good."

Everyone went back to working on their designated

tasks while music played in the background.

My phone vibrated and I smiled when I saw Memphis text me. I responded right back; butterflies filling my stomach when I hit send. Kym's pensive gaze caught my attention, making me aware of where I was at the moment. My smile dropped as I walked to the sink.

Beethoven's Fifth, also known as my mom's ringtone played and she excused herself to answer the call. I shook my head and dried my hands. Kym and I hated that ringtone and wish she would change it.

Kym joined me at the sink and nudged my side. "You seem… happy."

"I am happy."

She eyed me. "Yeah, but it's something making you this way."

With a shrug, I said, "Okay."

"Who were you texting earlier? And don't like and say Alex. She's never made you blush before."

I looked toward the door, hoping my mom wouldn't overhear anything.

"Swear not to say anything, and mean it, Kym." I shot her a glare that made her nod with fervor. "I met this guy like two weeks ago." I told her, shrugging to make light of the intense feelings I had for Memphis.

I'd met him two weeks ago and was in deep like. This feeling was weird, but I liked it. Kym looked at me like I had two heads.

"Is this the first man you've been with since Mark?"

While shaking my head, I replied, "No, but I actually *like* him too."

"Oh."

I didn't expect Kym to understand.

The chemistry I had with Memphis was beyond the physical. Yes, the sex was great, but I enjoyed being around him just as much. He was gentle, kind, and thoughtful.

I mean, I hadn't expected him to give me a picture of a butterfly after our first conversation, but the gesture meant so much. The photo made me smile every morning. It also made me think of him, which recently made me realize how much I like him.

"Now you know," I said to her after a second.

"Well, I'm happy for you. It's nice to see you're not totally jaded."

I smirked, then moved on to my next task. Kym stared at me for another second before moving on. I was sure she wanted to know more about Memphis. However, I wasn't ready to talk about him or us just yet.

We continued preparing dinner, then ate together like a regular family. My mom and I didn't fight. It had been a while since we enjoyed each other without any underlying tension coming forth. We were all getting used to our new normal as a family, but it was off to a good start.

After dinner, Kym brought out dessert. My dad sat next to me in the sunroom with a glint of curiosity in his eyes.

"What's on your mind, Dad?"

"The league loves your shirts, Kid. Another league outside of Hidden Lake wants your contact info. I told them I would talk to you about it."

My eyebrows hiked and I grinned. "How many teams are there?"

"Ten. Same as ours."

I did a quick calculation of how much profit I could make working with another league. And my dad's teammates were interested in other custom gear for their team. My business was flourishing right now.

"Send me their info," I told him.

He forwarded the email with the team's contact information.

"And Irene told me what happened with Mark." I nodded, waiting for him to say more. "How are you handling the news?"

I sighed. Having a dad who was a retired therapist sucked sometimes.

"I'm okay, Dad. Really."

"You'd tell me if you weren't?"

With a nod, I replied, "I would."

"Good," he said, then went back to eating his cake.

An hour later, I packed a bag of leftovers, and went home. During the drive home, I thought about getting a tattoo. My heart raced and I winced, thinking of the pain I might endure.

I waited I got home to look up tattoo ideas. By the time Memphis arrived, I had a design and an appointment at The Inkspot with Bellamy.

I grabbed my keys and met him in the garage.

"We're going to The Inkspot," I told him, unlocking my car. He nodded and hopped in the passenger's seat.

"What are you getting?" he asked, a few minutes into the ride.

I unlocked my phone and showed him a picture of three butterflies trailing over someone's wrist.

Memphis nodded. "Looks good. You scared?" he asked with humor in his tone.

"A little, but I'm trying not to think about it."

He chuckled. "You'll be aight."

A few moments later, we arrived at The Inkspot. After confirming my appointment at the front desk, Memphis and I looked through photobooks in the lounge area.

"You like this?" I asked showing him a lion tattoo.

He shrugged and continued sifting through his book.

"How was dinner?" I asked him.

Memphis shot me a half-smile, then said, "It was okay. I haven't spent the holidays with my family in a while. Being a part of their traditions are a reminder of how absent I've been. Tomorrow we're going to get a Christmas tree while Opal and my mom cook dinner, then we're decorating the tree and taking pictures. It's some shit out of a Hallmark movie."

I giggled because my family and I had a similar tradition. It sounds cheesy when telling people, but the experiences were truly unforgettable.

"It's not that bad, I promise."

Memphis didn't look too convinced. "Yeah, aight."

My tattoo artist, Bellamy came and introduced himself before taking us to his work suites. I was calm until Bellamy held the tattoo gun over my wrist. Memphis placed his hand on my knee.

"Wanna squeeze my hand?" He asked.

I grabbed his hand and closed my eyes. Upon the first line, I winced but remained still. My bottom lip was clenched between my teeth as Bellamy trailed the ink gun over my skin. I exhaled slowly, trying to calm my racing heart. Memphis's thumb caressed the back of my hand.

When Bellamy finished the tattoo, I couldn't stop looking at it. The three purple butterflies that trailed over my wrist were beautiful. After wiping my tattoo, he applied a derm shield to protect it. Memphis held the copies of sanitation and care forms as we left the shop. We walked Main Street looking for our next move.

"What are you in the mood for?" I asked him as we passed Cork & Easel. We'd been walking for a few blocks now.

"Walking is cool," he replied, reaching for my hand.

"Okay," I told him, then gave his hand a gentle squeeze.

We walked a few more blocks before crossing the street, then walking toward the car. Main Street was pretty busy tonight. It reminded me of how much of a homebody I'd become. Before going home, we stopped by an ice cream shop. We sat in the car while eating our ice cream, and talked about our childhoods. Our relationships with our parents and siblings were similar.

"My dad and Paris were always closer. The older I got the more my dad and I bumped heads. It's not as bad anymore because I've been away. We'll see how this week goes, though."

"It's the same with my family. My mom and I are a work in progress right now. When things were at their worst, my dad put basically became our therapist. It was an interesting time in our family."

My mom and I would probably never be like her and Kym, which was fine. Out personalities would never fully mesh. However, I wanted to reach a place where we didn't argue as much. And I wanted her to respect my boundaries.

My next relationship wouldn't be as open. I learned the importance of keeping somethings private. I'd want my family and future partner to be close, but not as close as they were with Mark. The lines had gotten so blurred that they made me feel like an outsider. I would be more cautious next time.

When we got home, I invited Memphis inside, hoping he'd stay the night. While he settled on the couch, I went to the bathroom, and checked on my tattoo. The butterflies were gorgeous and vibrant. I'm glad I took Memphis's advice and got color.

"You like it?" Memphis asked as I joined him on the couch.

"I love it."

Memphis held my arm while inspecting the tattoo. "Bellamy did his thing on this."

"He really did."

"What made you get it?"

"It was time. I finally feel like I'm about to become a butterfly."

My cheeks flushed at how corny it sound out loud, but it was true.

Memphis chuckled. "I feel you."

"I told my sister about you today," I said. "She saw me texting you and pressed me about it."

"What did you tell her?" Amusement bounced in his eyes, making my stomach flip.

"That I met someone, which was a big step because my dating life wasn't a topic, ever."

"My mom knows I met someone too. I didn't give her details because I don't want to deal with all the questions and pressure."

"Neither do I," I told him. "I like this though." I waved my hand between us.

Memphis moved closer to me, placing his arm around my shoulder, he said. "Me too."

I leaned in and captured his lips with mine. He cupped my cheek, deepening our kiss. My stomach tightened and heart fluttered from the gentle kisses he dropped along my chin and neck.

Memphis stopped kissing me and stared pensively.

"What's wrong?" I questioned.

He shook his head while a smile played on the corners of his mouth.

"I like you, Kiannah, and I don't want this to just be about sex."

"I know it's not," I replied with haste.

Memphis chuckled throatily. "That's not why I came here."

"Why'd you come?"

"I just wanted to be with you."

Heat coursed my veins from his admission. "You can stay as long as you want. I want to be around you too. As much as possible. Without sounding too clingy," I added.

"I get it."

Standing from the couch, I reached for his hand. Memphis placed his hand in mine and followed me upstairs.

He stood at the foot of the bed as I pulled his sweater over his head. Next, I removed his jeans. He sat down and watched me remove my clothes, then joined him in the bed.

I snuggled under his arm, inhaling his woodsy scented cologne and moaning. He laughed and tightened his hold on me. Memphis kissed my forehead sweetly making heat rush my cheeks.

"I like how I feel when I'm with you," I told him, breaking the silence between us.

Memphis sighed. The pads of his fingers tracing circles on my forearm, goosebumps covered my skin from his touch.

"I like how you make me feel," he replied. "Is it too soon?"

"No," I answered breathlessly.

"Good because I'm tired of trying to make sense of my feelings for you."

"Then don't."

Memphis brushed his nose against mine before kissing me. Soon our sweet kisses turned passionate.

"Stay," I told him when he pulled away.

Memphis kissed my nose. "I'm not going anywhere."

CHAPTER TWELVE

Memphis

Living a real-life Hallmark movie wasn't so bad. The ending wasn't as heartwarming as I imagined, though.

I waved bye to my parents as Paris backed out of the driveway to take them to the airport. The past week with my family had been long, and eye opening. My dad and Paris weren't as perfect as I thought. I'd overheard them arguing about Paris not wanting kids yet. I hadn't realized it was a point of contention for them.

Apparently, this wasn't the first time this was brought up. Their argument made me realize our dad was just an intrusive person, in general. Since then, Paris hadn't been in a mood.

After we bought the Christmas tree, Paris kept his distance from everyone. Later, I learned it was because Opal and my parents all felt the same about Paris's unreadiness to be a dad. Once Opal's parents were here, the tension wasn't as palpable. Their presence made everyone get their act together, and get along. However, I noticed that my dad and brother barely spoke to one another.

"You think Paris will be in a better mood now?" I asked Opal.

She shook her head. "I'm not sure. Their argument was pretty heated, I heard."

"It was. I didn't know whether I should've intervened or continue to stay away. I've never heard Paris raise his voice at our dad before," I said, recalling their tiff. "I hate that he let is ruin the entire week."

We walked inside to the kitchen.

"Me too, but that's just how he is. Maybe you could talk to him for me?"

My eyebrows met. "Yeah, and say what?"

"I don't know. But they're coming back in a few weeks for Christmas, and I refuse to deal with this tension."

"Let me know if I'm overstepping, but why doesn't he want kids yet?"

Opal sighed. "You brother has this idea of how he wants our family to look. And for him that can't happen until after he's running multiple businesses and I've gotten my Ph.D. I've tried to tell him it's possible for us to chase our dreams and have children. He just isn't seeing it that way."

"I get both sides," I told her.

"Me too, and I've accepted his stance on the matter. He lets Dad's opinion on the matter get him so upset to the point where it affects everyone," Opal's forehead wrinkled as she busied herself with the dishes in the sink.

I laughed because this was the exact conversation

Paris, and I had a few weeks ago. It looked like he needed to take his own advice for once.

"I'll talk to him," I told her after a beat.

She smiled. "Thank you."

I lingered in the kitchen while Opal cleaned.

"You don't have to sneak out anymore," she said, switching the subject.

With a chuckle, I replied, "I know. It was getting harder and harder to get away."

"You should've invited her over. Momma J would've loved to meet her."

"It's too soon, O. You know that."

"I mean, she wouldn't have caught you sneaking in had you brought her here."

The morning after I stayed with Kiannah, my mom bombarded me with questions. I hadn't expected her to go to the guest house first thing in the morning. But she did. She caught me slipping in quietly and knocked on the door. We had a nice talk about love and relationships. I finally opened up to her about my relationship with Nalia.

"She wouldn't have caught me if my sister had given me a heads up."

Opal giggled, splashing water on me. "Hey! I text you as soon as she asked about you."

She was right; however, I was asleep when she texted me. By the time I saw her message it was too late.

"How are things with Kiannah going?"

"We're good. Taking it slow and seeing how it goes."

Opal nodded. "Good, good. I like Kiannah for you."

Flashing a grin, I replied, "Me too."

After that night, me and Kiannah's relationship shifted. We were cool with taking it slow.

I was learning the journey was just as important as the destination.

———

LAWRENCE'S EYES widened while scrolling through my pictures on the screen.

"These are great man," he said after looking at the last photo. "I think these would be great for the exhibit."

I smiled, happy to see his response to what I had so far.

Hidden Lake had a snow day yesterday, and I spent the day capturing the winter wonderland. From Main Street to Heaven's Peak, I documented it all. Lawrence emailed me checking on the progress of my series, so I set up a time to meet with him.

"You'll have your work cut out for you when it's time to make final selections."

I pushed out a sigh. "I was hoping you'd help me out."

Lawrence chuckled. "How many do you have so far?"

"Close to five hundred. I'll narrow it down to two hundred soon."

"You done taking pictures?"

With a shrug, I replied, "For now."

Christmas was in a few days, and I knew I'd be too occupied with family events to work.

"Well, what you have so far, is great. There is still a little time to get more shots in if necessary. By February, you need to be editing the final pictures, and getting them printed. It'll be March before we know it," Lawrence said as he closed his laptop.

My heart raced as I thought about how little time I had. However, Lawrence was right, I had enough pictures to start the next phase of my project. I needed to get out my head and just flow.

After leaving our meeting, I went to meet Paris at The Oak Bar. With our parents coming today, I knew Paris was more tense that normal. We hadn't talked about the fight he had with our dad during Thanksgiving because I wanted to give him time to cool off. He'd been so focused on work lately, as I was with my photo series. The bar hadn't opened yet, so I didn't have to deal with the usual pat down and ID check at the door.

I nodded at security, then headed straight toward the bar. Behind it was a door leading to my brother's office. At the bar, a few waitresses, including Violet, were talking. When I got closer their conversation stopped and they stared.

"Hey, Memphis," Violet crooned while walking toward me.

I smirked, being polite, then said, "Wassup."

"Looking for Paris?"

"Yeah. Is he in his office?"

Violet shrugged, a grin forming on her mouth. "I don't know. Let's see."

The other waitresses giggled as she walked behind the bar with me.

"I haven't seen you in a minute," Violet noted as we walked down a narrow hallway.

"Not much of a bar person," I told her.

She nodded. "What have you been up to?"

"Working."

Violet stopped when we arrived at Paris's office. She leaned against the wall, stared at me.

"Are you still too good to take my number?" she purred.

I chuckled. "You know why I can't do that, right?"

Aside from not wanting to disrespect my brother, I was exclusively seeing Kiannah. Messing around with Violet would make our easy-going relationship complicated unnecessarily.

Violet kissed her teeth. "Okay," she said, rolling her eyes. I waited for her to exit the hall before knocking on the door of Paris's office.

I walked inside and laughed at the frustration on his face. His desk was covered with papers, and his computer.

"What's all of this?" I asked, taking a seat adjacent from him.

"End of year reports. I want all this shit handled before Christmas."

"You have a day or so," I teased him. "What time are you heading to the airport?"

Paris sighed. "I've been meaning to ask if you could go for me? I have too much here to stop right now."

My forehead wrinkled. Paris loved being the family chauffeur. The fight between him and our dad must've been worse than I thought.

"What did Dad do to have you avoiding him like this?"

Paris shook his head. "I'm not avoiding him." He held up a stack of papers. "I have to look through this and send it to my accountant today. Mom and Dad will be here in two hours."

I didn't fully believe him, but I decided to help him out.

"I got you man," I told him.

Paris bumped my fist with his. "I appreciate you, bro. How did the meeting go?" he asked, realizing why I came to see him.

"Great. Lawrence fucks with what I have so far. The winter wonderland shoot is my favorite thus far. It made me see Hidden Lake a little differently."

Paris grinned. "You're falling for its charm. I knew you would."

Hidden Lake had grown on me, I wasn't afraid to admit it anymore. I even started looking at apartments nearby. The possibility of signing a one-year lease was a big step for me, but I was easing into it.

Although it was too early to say if I wanted to stay, I was leaning toward living here for a while. I was growing to love being close to Paris and Opal. Also, Kiannah and I were getting closer each day. My feelings for her had me considering making it official.

"Something like that," I replied impishly. Before I left to get our parents, I had to talk to him for Opal. I couldn't risk our Christmas being like Thanksgiving. "You ready to tell me what happened with you and Dad?" I asked, measuring his disposition.

Paris dropped his pen and looked at me. "Dad is just being Dad. Overbearing, pushy, and stubborn. He doesn't get to say when I need to do when it comes to my family."

"Exactly," I told him. "So, why are you letting him get you this upset?"

"Because he thinks I'm a coward for wanting to wait to start a family. Me and Opal have a plan. There are things I want to accomplish, and Opal has some goals of her own. I don't want her to feel pressured into putting her dreams on hold to fulfill my parents' wishes. It's not fair to her."

"I thought she was ready?"

"She is, but their urgency is a major reason why. In private, she feels differently. It's my job to protect her, and I will. Even if that means not talking to the old man for a bit."

I nodded as his words settled. After listening to him, I understood his desire to protect his wife. I also needed him to realize that keeping the peace was also a form of protection for her.

"I agree with everything you're saying, but try to be cordial. When you're not in a good mood it affects everyone, even Opal. She can't host our parents, deal with your shitty mood, and stay in good spirits. It's not possible."

Paris chuckled. "I hear you."

"What was it you told me? Dad is stuck in his ways, and instead of trying to get him to see your point, you just gotta keep it pushing. He doesn't care to understand your viewpoint."

He stared at me with a grin. "So, you do listen?"

"Here and there. You should try it sometime."

"Man, whatever. I'll keep the peace for you and Opal."

My phone rang and I excused myself to answer. As I

walked down the hallway toward the exit, I smiled after hearing Kiannah's greeting.

"Hey, you," she crooned.

"I was just thinking about you," I told her.

She hummed. "Really? Because I was thinking about how you owe me another wine tasting."

I chuckled after remembering our bet. Kiannah had become the person to make team apparel thanks to her dad's bowling league. This past week, she got an order for twenty little league team shirts. She seemed overwhelmed by it but accepted the challenge with ease. She pressed seven shirts a day and finished ahead of schedule. I promised to take her to Cork & Easel if she met her deadline.

"I got you. When do you want to go?"

With Christmas coming up, I knew we'd be with our families. I couldn't risk my mom catching me coming home early in the morning again. It would be harder to maintain the lie that Kiannah was just a friend if I were seen coming from visiting her on Christmas.

"We can plan it after your parents leave. Opal told me about all the plans y'all have. Looks like you'll be living part two of a Hallmark movie."

"Yeah, I'm looking forward to the ugly Christmas sweater photo shoot though."

"Me too. Your sweater is the ugliest sweater I've ever seen." She giggled. "But remember the sweaters are better than the matching pajamas I'm wearing to the slumber party I'm having with my mom and sister."

We mocked our family traditions but loved to participate.

"I talk a lot of shit, but I'm happy to be here," I confessed.

This was the first year I truly felt the holiday spirit. All the corny traditions, and rituals made me feel closer to everyone. Knowing I had this to look forward to in the years to come made me want to stay in Hidden Lake for as long as possible.

We decided to wait until after Christmas to go out. Once we ended the call, I turned on music for my drive to the airport. As I thought about the memories this Christmas would bring, I smiled. After talking to Paris, I believed everyone would be able to get along, making my first Christmas back home an unforgettable one.

CHAPTER THIRTEEN

Kiannah

"How's editing going?" I asked Memphis, holding up the dress I bought for tonight.

The past two months he'd been shooting Hidden Lake for his upcoming exhibit. I was certain that he'd taken hundreds of pictures so far. Each showed the charm of my hometown.

"Good. I'm ahead of schedule," he said while clicking around on his computer.

"We need to leave soon," I reminded him.

Opal's birthday celebration was tonight at The Oak Bar. I knew Memphis was dragging his feet because he didn't want to go. He didn't like crowded spaces, which was basically The Oak Bar on most nights. I knew he wouldn't disappoint Opal by not showing up, though.

"Aight. I'm done for the night."

He closed his laptop and went to shower.

While he washed, I continued getting dressed. I checked the time on my phone before texting Alex. She arrived a few hours ago, and Lawrence picked her up from the airport. I was happy to hear they were going strong.

Alex had her fair share of bad boyfriends, and I knew she was ready to settle down. Hopefully, Lawrence would be the one to sweep her off her feet. So far, he had already impressed her by sending flowers twice a month and going to visit her.

An hour later, we arrived at The Oak Bar. Opal and Trinity were already tipsy by the time we arrived. Opal gave us shot upon arrival, making us take them before we could greet everyone.

"Happy birthday," I said while hugging her.

Memphis handed her the flowers we'd bought, then they shared an embrace. I looked around the VIP section and recalled sitting in this exact spot the night I met Memphis.

"Remember this table?" He said against the shell of my ear.

My stomach flipped and cheeks warmed.

"Yes, I remember."

Memphis kissed my forehead, then grabbed my waist. "You were acting all shy in your tight black dress."

I couldn't help my grin as he recalled the night we met. I remembered the dress and heels I wore that night. Alex suggested I wear the dress as a part of her grand plan for me to meet someone. When she got here, I'd have to thank her for her part in me meeting Memphis.

"I was not acting shy!" I pushed his shoulder while giggling.

Memphis closed the space between us, peering down at me. Lust gleamed in his eyes, making heat course my veins. It had been a few weeks since we last had sex. He was busy working on his exhibit and we hadn't spent much time together. I had a feeling that wouldn't be the case tonight, though.

Memphis smirked. "You weren't shy when we got back to my place."

"Let me know when you're ready to go back."

He leaned down and kissed me. My heart raced, and pussy throbbed from his passionate kisses. For a second, I forgot where we were. Opal had no problem reminding us when she said, "Get a room," making everyone laugh.

A few minutes later, Alex and Lawrence arrived, taking the party up a notch. She happily accepted Opal's mandatory shots and started dancing. I knew Memphis wouldn't mind staying at the table, so I joined my girls on the dance floor. About three songs in, I paused, realizing how much fun I was having. I couldn't recall the last time I partied with my friends. The thought made me smile.

I was genuinely happy with life right now.

Any day now, my divorce would be finalized, my business was exceeding my expectations, and I'd met someone that I could see myself with for the long haul.

The DJ switched the song, snapping me from my trance. I went upstairs to check on Memphis and get another drink. As I neared the table, heat coursed my veins as I watched Memphis flirt with the waitress.

She was bent over, whispering in his ear while he nodded. I wasn't sure what she was saying, but the way she rubbed his shoulder led me to believe she wasn't taking his order. I stalked over to them, catching Memphis attention.

He reached for me hand, and I pulled it away from him. The waitress smiled sweetly and asked if I needed anything.

"We're good," I told her, folding my arms over my chest.

I didn't know her name, but I remembered seeing her all over Memphis the night we met.

"What's that about?" I asked once she was gone.

Memphis's eyebrows met as he pulled me onto his lap. "What do you mean?"

"You and her."

My blood was boiling. I hadn't realized how triggering it would be to see him talking to another woman. I took a deep breath, and reminded myself that Memphis wasn't Mark. He hadn't given me any reason not to trust him.

"She's not important," was his reply before he kissed my neck. "I'm not worried about her, babe."

I looked at Memphis, and immediately felt guilty for overreacting.

"You good?" he asked when I didn't respond to his kisses.

I nodded. "Yeah, seeing you with her just made me spiral a bit."

"I get it, and I apologize for how it might've looked. But I promise you have nothing to worry about. You're the only one I want, Kiannah." he punctuated his statement with a sweet kiss, bringing me back to reality.

Memphis was unlike Mark which was what attracted me to him. I hated how these irrational fears crept up on me. Memphis didn't seem phased by my mini tantrum. In fact, he stayed close to me all night, reminding me that I was who he wanted. The past three months with him had been nothing less than what I deserved.

"Have I told you how good you look tonight?" Memphis asked while I swayed my hips on him. He placed his hands on both sides of me as I peered downstairs at the people at the bar.

"Yes. Like a million times," I replied, while playfully rolling my eyes. I was playing coy, but my heart was racing a mile minute from his closeness. "You can keep telling me though."

Memphis chuckled. "You're something else, Kiannah."

Turning in his arms, I faced him. The desire filling his orbs had me pressing me body deeper into his.

"So are you."

He looked at me, his eyes narrowing as he licked his lips. "You ready to go?"

"We can't leave yet."

"Why not?" he pressed, gripping my ass.

I smirked. "Because it's only been like an hour. It's not officially Opal's birthday yet."

Memphis checked the time on his phone. "Aight, but we're leaving our we sing happy birthday."

"Deal."

About thirty minutes later, Paris came out with a cake and bottles for his wife. Everyone sang to Opal while she blushed and clapped along. She closed her eyes and made a wish before blowing out the candles. I smiled watching Opal and Paris embrace one another.

Memphis hugged me from behind. "You ready to go now?"

"Yes," I told him, feeling his hardened dick against my ass.

"Good," he said, dropping torturing kisses along my neck. My body hummed from his touch.

After saying bye to everyone, we went back to his place. It didn't take long for our clothes to be on the ground once we got there. Memphis was gently but till moved with urgency when leading me to his bed.

I USED to hate Valentine's Day.

It was a day Mark used to overcompensate for all his previous indiscretions. All the balloons, roses, and gifts were painful reminders of the ways he wronged me.

Snap out of it.

Memphis planned an evening for us to celebrate the holiday. I hadn't told him I'd rather stay in and watch a movie because I didn't want to seem like a mood killer. Plus, it was rare for a man to be into this holiday. It obviously meant a lot to him to go to dinner, and exchange gifts. I didn't want to ruin that for him.

The doorbell rang, and I shook away all the thoughts racing my mind.

As I opened the door for Memphis, I pushed out a breath.

He handed me two dozen long stemmed roses, with a notecard attached. I stepped aside giving him room to come inside. After closing the door, I opened the card and smiled.

CHAPTER 13

Will you be my valentine, indefinitely?
Yes, no, or maybe.
-Memphis

When I looked up from the card, he was waiting for my response.

"Yes," I said, running over to him.

I kissed him sweetly before stepping back to admire my flowers. It was so cute the way he asked me to be his girlfriend. We hadn't talked about becoming officially, but it felt like we already were. We talked everyday, and he spent the night a few times a week.

We seamlessly fit into each other's life, reinforcing the instant attraction I had to him. This moment was all the more special, because I received the official notice finalizing my divorce.

Valentine's Day was slowly becoming one of my favorite days, again.

"What time is our reservation?" I asked, hurrying upstairs to grab my boots and purse.

"We have some time." He followed me upstairs to me bedroom. "Lawrence and I finalized the pictures for the exhibit today."

I met his smile with one of my own. "Really? How many? And did you choose my favorite one?"

"We decided on ten, and yes, I made sure to include the sunset."

Wrapping my arms around his neck, I pecked his lips before hugging him.

I didn't have the words to express how proud I was of Memphis. For months, he worked on this series tirelessly.

He was almost at the end of the road, and I couldn't wait to see his vision materialized.

"The next month is all about promoting me and my exhibit. I'm having dinner with the board members, and director of museum next week. And I have several interviews to do too."

"Are you excited?"

Memphis nodded. "Honestly, it's reminding me how much I loved the press run for my book."

"Maybe you can start that once this dies down?"

Memphis expressed his desire to start his next book. We stayed up one night and went through his archives. Without planning to he figured out his next book idea; a collection of portraits.

"Yeah, Loren will be here for the opening. We'll talk more about it then."

I put on my other boot, then went to the bathroom to look over my appearance. My haircut had grown out, and I was debating if I wanted to trim it. But for now, I loved that I could tuck my hair behind my ear again.

Memphis came behind me while I checked my appearance. He held out a black velvet box, making me smile.

"What's this?" I mused.

He's the sweetest.

I held up the silver necklace with a butterfly pendant, and gasped.

"It's gorgeous!"

Memphis took the necklace from me, and placed it around my neck. I ran my fingers across the diamond encrusted butterfly pendant.

"Thanks, baby," I told him, turning around.

I hopped on the bathroom counter, spreading my legs wide enough for him to come closer. He kissed me ardently, while slipping his hands underneath my blouse.

But what about dinner?

I knew we had reservations soon, but I didn't care anymore. Judging by the way Memphis was kissing me, he didn't care either. He slipped my blouse over my head, then continued kissing me like he had something to prove. Once I felt his hands at the button of my jeans, I moved the counter to push them over my waist.

Memphis turned me around to face the mirror, then unbuckled his pants. I handed him a condom from the drawer after pushing down my panties. He slid into me, making my stomach stir and mouth open. I arched my back deeper, relishing in the feeling of his girth in me.

I watched our bodies in the mirror. Memphis's gaze met mine and my heart fluttered from the fire in his eyes. I gripped the counter for support as he drove into me, hitting the exact spot to have juices running down my legs.

Outfit ruined.

Memphis used his knee to spread my legs wider as he quickened his strokes. I bit my bottom lip thing my hardest to hold back my moans. He chuckled throatily, gripping my waist tighter. A rolling sensation shot through my belly and my eyes closed tightly.

My body felt tingly and heart raced as an orgasm ripped through me. I leaned over and met his strokes, aiding him to his peak. He kissed my shoulders and neck while I fought to catch my breath. For seconds, we stared at each other in the mirror. A smile playing on my lips when my gaze landed on my necklace.

"We can still make dinner," Memphis said, his hoarse chords sent a chill down my spine. "I mean, if you're up for it."

I smirked, still looking at him through the mirror.

"Only if you promise there will be dessert."

Memphis flashed a half-smile. "Always, baby," he said, slapping my ass.

I pushed him out of the bathroom and cleaned up. We had a small window before out dinner plans would be canceled. After changing my pants, I went back to the bathroom, to touch up my makeup. As I put away my eyeshadow, I stopped and admired the butterfly picture Memphis gave me.

I was finally being treated the way I deserved by a man I adored more than anything. Six months ago, I didn't think I'd find someone and click so soon.

Now, I had everything I yearned for during my marriage. But it felt ten times better coming from Memphis because I didn't have to beg for it. He gave me everything I needed and more, without even trying.

As we drove to dinner, I caught myself smiling uncontrollably. Memphis caught it too. Reaching for my hand, he brought it to his lips.

Best Valentine's Day ever.

CHAPTER FOURTEEN

Memphis

Home by the Lake.

I smiled as I read the title to my series posted above three of my pictures. A year ago, I was in Portugal struggling to meet my publisher's needs. Today, I was at the opening of my exhibit with my family, and lady. The reminder of how quickly life can change made me feel an immense amount of gratitude.

Kiannah slipped her hand into mine as she came beside me.

"My favorite picture," she mused, staring at the picture of Heaven's Peak in the center of the three photos.

"Mine too," my mom said, standing on the other side of me.

I brought Kiannah's hand to my mouth and kissed it.

"This is my lady, Kiannah," I told my mom who was smiling from ear to ear.

She pushed me aside and hugged Kiannah lovingly. "It's nice to finally meet you, sweetie. I've been waiting ever since I caught him sneaking home back in November."

Kiannah's cheeks reddened. "It's nice to meet you too, Mrs. Jarreau."

I wanted to stay and talk to the two most important ladies in my life, but Lawrence needed me to mingle a few of the museums most valuable donors. Apparently, my exhibit was something they'd been wanting for years.

I spent the next hour schmoozing as we waited for more guests to arrive. Every free second I had, I spent looking around the gallery. Tonight's turnout was far greater than my first showing many years ago. I got a little emotional thinking about my mentor. I wished he was alive to see how far I'd come. I knew he would be proud of me.

"Son," my dad called out, snapping me out of my thoughts. "This is nice."

My eyes widened and head tilted to the side. "Which one do you like the most?" I questioned as we walked past two pictures.

He walked me over to the two pictures I chose from the winter wonderland shoot. He pointed at the shot I took of Main Street covered in a blanket of snow. Many of the business were closed for the day, and there were people building snowmen in the streets.

"It reminds me of my childhood in upstate when we had snow days."

I nodded. "I'm glad you like it, Dad."

He scanned the room, looking at the other photos I had on the walls.

"You're talented, son. I'm not just saying that either."

With a chuckle, I replied, "I know. When do you ever say things just because."

My dad's chuckle made me grin. I knew this was close to sentimental as we would ever get. Knowing at least one of my images touched him was enough for me.

"Memphis, can I steal you for a moment?" Lawrence tapped my arm.

My dad motioned for me to go with Lawrence, then he continued view the exhibit.

"This is Paul Morris, an editor at Mountain Living Magazine. He saw your pictures and wants to do a feature on Hidden Lake through your lens."

I shook Paul's hand, and he immediately went into his spiel. By the end of our conversation, we'd set up a meeting for next week. After wrapping up with Paul, I searched the room for Kiannah. I couldn't wait to share this news with her.

My search was disrupted when Loren spotted me from across the room.

"Memphis!" She shrieked, making me laugh. "Everything is beautiful. I see your camera kept you busy these last few months."

"I found my sweet spot."

Loren nodded. "Indeed you did. I want to introduce you to Isaac."

"Nice to meet you," Isaac said.

We shook hands, then jumped right into my exhibit.

"I loved your book, too," he said as we strolled around the gallery. "You prefer landscape photography these days, huh?"

I shook my head. "I wanted to try something new. I learned that helps when I'm feeling uninspired."

"I see."

We continued looking at the pictures, and I took a few moments to explain each one.

"In your book, you had quite a few portraits. I liked those."

My eyebrows shot up. "Me too. I wanted to add more, but my former publishers didn't want me to, and they used focus groups to reinforce their wants."

Isaac's mouth twisted as he looked over the last picture in my series.

"Yeah, I hear Array Publications isn't the most collaborative company. It's their way or no way."

"Hence why I'm no longer with them."

Isaac chuckled while nodding. "Sounds like you had luck on your side, huh? If that hadn't happened, you wouldn't have this beautiful showcasing of your work, am I right?"

"You are."

"And, we wouldn't have met either. If you're interested, we'd love to publish your next book," he told me.

A smile spread across my face as I accepted his offer. "Absolutely."

"Great, I'll talk to Loren about getting you to LA for a meeting soon."

"Sounds like a plan to me," I said, shaking his hand.

I could hardly contain my excitement after talking to Isaac. To think four months ago, I didn't know where my life or career was headed. Tonight, I was offered a deal and a feature in a magazine.

"You're a hard man to find," Kiannah said, strolling over to me. I was on the opposite side of the gallery trying to collect my thoughts. My adrenaline was pumping through my veins at rapid speed.

"Babe, I have so much good news to share with you when we get home."

"Home?" She questioned with a hiked brow. "Yours or mine?"

"Where we are is home," I replied, smiling when her Sienna colored skin flushed. From across the room, Lawrence waved his hand, and held up a microphone. "Let me give closing remarks, and I'll tell you everything when we leave."

She nodded, then kissed my cheek.

I walked over to Lawrence and faced the crowd to speak.

"I just want to thank everyone for coming out tonight. This series means a lot to me. I came to Hidden Lake a few months ago, with no plan and honestly, no desire to stay long. However, I couldn't resist the town's charm. Each picture depicts something I love about this town. From the mountainous views to Main Street the town has so much character and deserves the spotlight."

The crowd clapped, giving me a moment to gather my thoughts.

"I want to thank Lawrence and the rest of the board for allowing me to do this series. You all trusted my vision and I think we did a good job."

Lawrence nodded while holding up his drink. "To Memphis Jarreau and Home by the Lake."

Everyone who had a drink toasted to me before clapping. I spent the next half hour thanking the guests who stayed until the end, and taking pictures.

By the time I left, I was too tired to do anything else but cuddle with Kiannah on her couch.

"Remember what you said earlier about going home?"

I smirked, then said, "Yeah."

"You consider Hidden Lake your home?"

"Yes, and you too."

"How long do you plan on staying? I know the exhibit was one reason you haven't left yet."

I met Kiannah's pensive gaze. "I don't have any plans on leaving, I found another reason to stay."

Her eyebrows shot up. "Oh, why?"

"You."

Kiannah's eyes lit up, and cheeks reddened. I pulled her onto my lap and kissed her cheek, neck, then her lips. Kiannah was the best thing to happen to me. Throughout this journey, she remained beside me and encouraged me along the way. There were plenty of nights where I wanted to give up, but she kept the going.

The only way I planned on leaving was if she came with me, until then I'd be here with her.

EPILOGUE

Kiannah

Memphis squeezed my hand while we waited for Kym to open the door. My heart raced with every passing second. Moments later, she opened the door, and smiled politely.

"Kym, this my boyfriend, Memphis." I looked at him. "This is my sister, Kym."

Kym opened her arms. "It's nice to finally meet you. I've heard a lot about you."

Seeing them embrace warmed my heart. For weeks, I obsessed over introducing Memphis to my family. We'd been together for almost five months, and I'd grown tired of keeping him to myself.

"Nice to meet you too. Key talks about you and your cooking all the time."

"Well, come inside so you can see what the hype is about," Kym said, laughing.

I grabbed his hand again as we walked through the foyer and through the kitchen. My heart pounded against my chest when I met my dad's gaze.

"Hey, Kid," he said, glancing at Memphis before hugging me. "You must be Memphis?" my dad held out his hand for Memphis to shake.

"That's right. Nice to finally meet you," Memphis said, getting a smile from my dad.

I held his hand tighter, feeling a little overprotective of him. I knew my dad would give him the third degree, and I didn't want Memphis to become overwhelmed. I was just in his shoes a month before at the viewing of his exhibit.

I told my dad I was dating again to gauge his reaction before telling him I was in a relationship. He seemed relived to hear that I had moved on from Mark. My dad also noted a change in my mood since I started seeing Memphis. I guess I wasn't as secretive as I thought.

"Let's talk before dinner," my dad said to Memphis.

I assumed he wanted to have "the talk" with him. Memphis glanced over his shoulder, winking at me as they left the kitchen.

Kym looked at me with wide eyes once we were alone.

"He's cute," she beamed. "This is the guy from the bar a few months back?"

I nodded. "Yup. That's him."

"I don't have to ask if he's treating you right. It's all over you. I haven't seen you like this in years."

My eyes watered from my sister's accurate assessment. I hadn't planned on falling for him so soon, but I didn't regret it. This feeling was new, but exhilarating, and I wanted to ride it for a long as possible.

I heard the heels of my mom's boots tapping against the floors, and my heart raced instantly.

This is the real test.

My mom and I had been doing great the past few months. She knew I was dating, but didn't overstep by asking too many questions. I assured her I would introduce Memphis when I was ready.

"Hey, baby," she said, hugging me.

"I have someone I want you to meet."

I didn't tell that I was bringing Memphis ahead of time in case she overreacted. Taking her by the hand, I led her to the sunroom where Dad and Memphis were laughing. Seeing their interaction warmed my heart and lessened my fears of bringing Memphis around my family.

"Memphis, this is my mom." He stood and held out his hand, unsure of how'd she greet him.

When my mom rolled her eyes, then held out her arms, I exhaled.

"Come here, boy," she said, hugging him. "You're the one who has my daughter smiling all the time."

Memphis smirked at me, making me roll my eyes.

"I see why you wanted to keep him to yourself," she leaned over and said to me. "He is truly tall, dark, and handsome."

"Behave, Ma."

She held up her hands in defense. "I'm just saying."

We talked a little about Memphis's career while waiting for dinner to be ready. I knew my parents were saving the deep questions for dinner. I was a bit nervous to hear what they had to say about him, but so far it seemed like my parents were feeling Memphis.

"Dinner's ready," Kym said moments later, prompting us to all go to the dining room.

Memphis's eyes widened when he saw the spread Kym had prepared for tonight.

"She does this twice a month?"

I nodded. "Yup. Now, you see why I rarely miss dinner."

"I do. She and Opal need to meet."

"I keep saying that. We need to make it happen."

Once everyone was seated, my dad blessed the food, then we ate. Kym dominated the conversation by talking about her upcoming wedding. She and Everett had finally set a date. No one was more excited than our mom who already had a wedding planner and venue on standby.

"So, Memphis," my mom said when Kym stopped talking. "Are you an only child?"

He shook his head. "No, I have an older brother named Paris. I've been staying with him and my sister-in-law for a few months now."

She nodded. "And your parents?"

"Still together, living in upstate New York."

"Are you close with them?"

I shot her a look that she ignored. I knew she was asking because of Mark was estranged from his family. She knew I didn't want her to compare the two.

"Yeah, we are a close knit family," he answered, honestly.

"Good. Family is very important to us."

Memphis nodded. "I know. Kiannah talks about y'all often and she doesn't play when it comes to these dinners. I'm glad I was finally invited."

Everyone laughed.

"We're happy you're here too," Kym said.

EPILOGUE 151

My mom continued giving Memphis the third degree, but didn't ask anything too personal. He answered each question without hesitating. When my mom found out he used to live abroad, she talked about how she used to travel before she got married. It was nice hearing her stories about living in Spain. She and Memphis compared their experiences.

By the time we left dinner, I felt like a weight was lifted off my shoulders. Memphis and my family meshed well together. And I knew it was genuine because Kym text me as soon as I left her house.

"Your family is cool," he said as we got ready for bed.

I shrugged. "They're okay when they want to be," I joked. "I'm glad everyone likes you."

"Your mom *loves* me."

I giggled while snuggling under him. "Right. I had to remind her that her man was sitting next to her."

Memphis chuckled, then kissed my forehead.

"But seriously, thank you for agreeing to come. I've been stressing over this day for weeks. I would've been crushed had things not gone well."

"I would've done whatever it took to win them over."

"Really? Why?"

"I know how important your family unit is to you." He passed, staring deeply into my eyes.

" And because, I love you."

Memphis dropped a sweet kiss on my lips, making my heart flutter.

"I love you, too."

More than he knew.

THE END

Thank you for taking the time to read Alone With You!

Please consider leaving a review on Amazon and/or Goodreads.

Until next time,

D.

ACKNOWLEDGMENTS

Asia and Shanice, "we did it Joe!"
CCJ, you're top two and not two!
To my readers, thank you for remaining loyal during this time.

ALSO BY D. ROSE

Fire & Desire:

Love Me Up

Take You Down

For Keeps:

New Year Kiss (A Short Story)

Because of Love

The Sweetest Love

On Love's Time

Roseville:

Brown Sugar

Ready for Love

Second Chance:

Another Chance to Love

All I Need is You

The Boos and Booze Series:

Brewing Storm (#6)

The Luminous Cruise Chronicles:

Love Overboard (#3)

Standalone Titles:

Cherie Amour

Yearning for Your Love

True Love for Christmas

Milk & Honey: a collection of shorts

Love's Language

Warmth

Share My World

Pieces of Love

Love on Repeat

My One Christmas Wish

A New Year With You

The Vow

Together Again

Made in the USA
Columbia, SC
20 November 2024